Song of the Jackalope

BY

ROY CAMPBELL

(BABA ROY)

Song of the Jackalope

BY

ROY CAMPBELL

(BABA ROY)

Illustrations by David Bosworth

Layout by Terry Sherrell

Song of the Jackalope
Published by Bridgeway Books
2100 Kramer Lane, Suite 300
Austin, Texas 78758

For more information about our books, please write to us, call 512.478.2028, or visit our website at www.bookpros.com.

Printed and bound in China.

Library of Congress Control Number: 2005931611

ISBN-13: 978-1-933538-04-4
ISBN-10: 1-933538-04-X

To Lauren, Alexander and Noah

This book is dedicated to you and others who are still young. As you grow older, may you always keep a place in your hearts for the jackalope's song and all that it means.

With much love,
Baba Roy

". . . There's music in the sighing of a reed;
There's music in the gushing of a rill;
There's music in all things, if men had ears;
Their earth is but an echo of the spheres. . . ."

From *Don Juan, Canto the Fifteenth,*
by George Gordon Byron

Table of Contents

Author's Foreword

One late summer day when I was about seven years old, an itinerant book salesman came to our door. It was a time when money was scarce in my family, and the clouds of war were gathering for our nation. But on that day, my father and mother made one of the wisest purchases that I can ever recall them making. When the man left, it was with a signed order for a twelve-volume set of *My Book House*, edited by Olive Beaupre Miller. The arrival of those books brought to our household a world of marvelous literature for children. In those pages, I often found joy by stretching the boundaries of my imagination and wandering through strange realms that seemed exciting and wonderful. For me, it was an opportunity for enrichment, belied by the frequently difficult circumstances of my family's everyday life.

Now as an older adult, I step gingerly back into the arena of children's stories. By writing *Song of the Jackalope,* it is my hope to make a small contribution to the vast wealth of material that already exists for children. Perhaps some of the readers of this book, both young and old, will find a measure of identity with little Molly Jackalope. One may empathize with certain of her feelings, her dreams, her fears and that experience of exaltation that can flood the heart and soul on occasion. Also within the jackalope community, there are unabashed allusions to other humanlike equalities that most of us will recognize. As for the jackalope itself, there has been a dearth of literature and information about this legendary creature. So, my plunge into the nearly vacant space has been taken with a great deal of freedom and license, not to mention a healthy degree of pure enjoyment, too.

Without the superb illustrations by David Bosworth, this book would not have become a reality. The drawings do more than present simple pictures. They enter the spirit of the story at every juncture. Having absolutely no artistic ability myself, I am deeply grateful for David's talent and for our excellent working relationship. That kind of relationship also developed with David Stanton, who did the layout for the first edition. Truly, it takes a team to produce a book.

Finally, it is noted that elements of the story are tinged with the supernatural (not saturated, just tinged). There is within all of us, I believe, a vague yearning for the mystical, for the world created by imagination that transcends the confines of practical reality. However, the primary thrust of the story itself is not about magic. Its principal character, Molly, is a very ordinary little creature. But as the plot develops, it is not without some rather mysterious happenings. A few hints are given about possible sources and causes, but much is left to the interpretation of the reader. I merely wrote the story.

Song of the Jackalope

On a western hillside, a pack of hungry coyotes flushed their prey from a thicket of scrub mesquite. With gleeful yips, they began pursuing what first appeared to be a large jack rabbit. But what was this thing? In between its long ears, the animal was sporting a set of small antlers similar to those of an antelope. Darting first to the left, and then to the right, it reached the bottom of the hill where it put on a burst of speed and quickly outran the trailing coyotes. Once at a safe distance, the creature stopped, turned around and emitted several coyote-like yips in a rude mockery of its hapless pursuers. The sounds seemed to linger tauntingly upon the air as the discouraged pack abandoned the chase. From this small episode, the artful and elusive jackalope emerged from the shadows of an Old West legend. With a certain air of amusement, it bounded onto these pages for the entertainment of the reader.

Many years ago, cowboys sitting around their campfires at night would occasionally hear a sound like someone singing out on the prairie. They would recognize the sound as the song of a jackalope and could tell by the type of music if all was well with their cattle herd. A happy little melody meant there was no lurking danger, the air was calm and the desert, night sky was clear with a host of stars and a watchful moon. But a melody with sudden starts and stops was taken as a warning. There might be a pack of coyotes or wolves ready to pounce on the young calves in the cattle herd. Or a big thunderstorm might be coming, meaning that the cowboys would have to use their ponchos like tents to keep the rain off. The cowboys didn't have to see the jackalope to know it was there—just listen to its song.

During that time, in the desert foothills southeast of Thunder Mountain, Molly Jackalope lived in a small village with her family. She was two years old, which was about like being a teenager in jackalope years. But Molly was small for her age. Due to a collision with a large cactus plant when she was almost one, she had lost one of her antlers. She wasn't able to run as fast as the other young jackalopes. When she did run, she would tend to veer off a little to the side where her one antler was located, always a bit off balance. Because of her physical differences, Molly was often left behind

when the other jackalopes went out at night looking for cowboys and their campfires.

Once they found what they were looking for, the older jackalopes would always sing their songs as good jackalopes were supposed to do. But some of the younger jackalopes were mischievous and would make noises like frogs croaking around a pond, or like a baby crying. That would cause the cowboys to rush out into the darkness trying to find the source of the unusual sound. Then the young jackalopes would hop away into the night, giggling and chuckling to each other.

One evening, an old man came into the territory where Molly's family lived. His name was Henry. He was not a cowboy, and he did not have a horse. Years before, Henry had become separated from his family and decided to become a sheepherder. So now, he walked with a donkey carrying his pack and with a flock of sheep to wherever they were able to find food. It was a lonely life. At times, Henry did not see other people for several weeks. There was no radio, television or newspapers, so he had to depend on his animals and nature to provide him with entertainment. He had found many pleasures living out on the plains and in the gentle hills under an open sky. When he wasn't busy with his animals, he might watch a hawk soaring high in the sky, or listen to the sound wind made as it whispered among the rocks and the desert plants.

In the daytime, there were often jack rabbits hopping about and antelopes grazing in the distance. Occasionally,

a few buffalo might wander nearby. At night, as Henry snuggled under a wool blanket, the dark sky above would be littered with lights from a thousand stars and from the mysterious moon. The sheep would nestle down, quiet except for a soft "*baaa*" when a mother would call to a wayward lamb. When the lamb returned to its mother, all would be quiet again.

On the day Henry, along with his flock and donkey, wandered into jackalope territory, the old man walked with a bowed head and a heavy step. A few days before, Sorene, his only sheepdog, had died. She had been with him for many years, faithfully keeping any of the sheep from straying, and guarding his flock at night. The man and dog were close companions, and Henry had felt secure knowing his faithful helper was always there. As she became older, Sorene had begun to move more slowly, frequently walking instead of running to head off a wayward lamb. On her last day, the old dog had spied a coyote among the rocks on a nearby hill. Away she went, running as fast as she could to drive the coyote back and protect the sheep. Henry, climbing up the rocks behind her, found his old companion behind a large boulder. She was dead; her heart had stopped from the sudden strain.

Overcome with shock and great sorrow, Henry sat beside Sorene's body for a long time. Finally, he arose, and with tears still in his eyes, he gathered rocks, placing them over her body, creating a burial mound. Then slowly, he had made his way back down the hill to rejoin his donkey and the grazing sheep.

Now, they had all come to a small stream where the patient donkey and all the sheep stopped and gratefully sipped from the cool water. The old man looked around. This would be a good place to rest for a few days he decided. There seemed to be a lot of grass growing in clumps near the stream that would be excellent for the animals. On the other side of the stream, a small, rocky ridge extended back toward the nearby mountains. On his side, there was a large plain with small hills visible in the distance. Perhaps, Henry thought as he started gathering firewood, this quiet place would help him overcome some of the sadness he felt. He did feel a little nervous about the coyotes coming at night. Without Sorene to bark, he might not wake up in time and some of the little lambs would be in danger. But both he and the animals were weary from all their travel. The place he had chosen would have to be their temporary home. So the sheepherder gathered up firewood, and that night he built a campfire.

On the same day that the sheepherder arrived in the area, Molly Jackalope was hopping along, in her usual awkward manner, into a small canyon. There were bunches of grass growing among the scattered desert flowers, shrubs and Piñon trees where she was, and the little jackalope began having an afternoon meal. She felt safe from coyotes there, although she was alone. Actually Molly had wanted to get away from

the other young jackalopes who were always making jokes about her. They called her "Molly Half-a-Lope" and "Dope-a-Long Bunny," along with a lot of other mean names.

There was another reason Molly often chose to be alone, away from the others. One of the unique things about jackalopes is their ability to sing. It is said that even a very young jackalope can make several musical sounds with its voice. Molly's voice, however, was a little different from those of the other jackalopes. It was at times softer, but with a frequent lilt, like the sound of a flute. Because she was alone so much, Molly hadn't learned many of the songs the others knew. But she would listen to the sounds of a small brook, or of birds singing, and try to include these in little melodies that she made up for herself. Some were happy tunes, but often, the melody would express sorrow because Molly felt sad at times. Once secluded away in the little canyon, she could practice these melodies and songs without the others hearing and without being teased. So it was sundown on this day before she stopped singing and decided to leave the little canyon for home. After coming out of the entrance, the jackalope saw something unusual. In the darkening twilight, she could see a flickering light some distance away. What could it be out there where there had not been a light before?

After supper, Henry sat by his fire and gazed into the yellow flames. Finally, he turned and looked out over the darkened plain. It almost seemed that he could hear Sorene giving occasional little barks to let him know that all was well as she trotted around the resting flock of sheep. But listening again, the only real sounds he heard were those of sheep shifting about and the murmur of a soft, desert wind in the night. So with a sigh, Henry stood up and went over to his backpack. He took out a small flute and brought it back to his place by the fire. There had been happy times, and some sad times in Henry's life before he decided to become

a sheepherder. When playing the flute, it was almost as if he was reliving some of those times. Tonight, his present sorrow and loneliness were evident in the mournful sound of his music. The notes seemed to echo off the rocks on the nearby ridge and drift hauntingly out among the shadows away from the campfire. There were no other human ears to hear, which reassured the flute player somewhat as he directed his music into the solitude of the night itself.

But there WERE other ears listening. About a mile away, a pair of coyotes was exploring a prairie dog village, sniffing about in hopes of catching one of the little animals out of its burrow. Hearing the faint, musical strains of the flute on the night air, they lifted their heads for a moment in the direction of the sound. Then, both coyotes decided to ignore what they heard and resumed their search for some prairie-dog supper.

Much closer to the campfire, two other listening ears belonged to a young jackalope crouching behind some sagebrush. It was Molly. She had decided to investigate the cause of the flickering light she had seen. As she came closer, the campfire's glow in the darkness had been a magnet, pulling her in a way that was irresistible. Now, here it was, the music that had caused the little jackalope to finally creep up even closer to the spot where she was now hiding. It was almost as if the man and the flute were talking directly to her. She felt his sadness as he played. The voice of the flute spoke to her little heart in a way that music had never done before.

Crouching behind the sagebrush, Molly wished there was some way she could talk back and answer the sounds the flute was making. She longed to somehow help the player and bring comfort to him for his sadness, but she felt quite small and inadequate. So after listening a bit longer, the little jackalope hopped quietly away into the darkness.

For the next three nights, Molly returned to the scene of Henry's campfire and sat watching and listening. But there was no more flute music. After his supper, the old man would simply sit by the fire, sometimes standing up to get another stick of firewood or to go out and check on his sheep. There was always a weariness in his manner. With the desert nights becoming colder, it would soon be time to move on and take the flock south to where the weather would be warmer. He realized the need to do that, but somehow lacked the will and the energy to start the journey. Besides, there seemed to be something strangely attractive about this place, but for what reason, he was not sure.

On the fourth day, Molly decided not to go back to the man's camp for a while. There really wasn't anything she could do to help him, she thought. Besides, she had her own troubles to worry about. You see, much of the time, Molly felt sorry for herself. She envied the other jackalopes who didn't have a missing antler. Also, they knew all of the popular songs to sing to the cowboys at night. She knew her voice was different from theirs and felt it was useless to try and learn those songs. So on this day, Molly wandered morosely back into her little canyon as she had done many times before.

About halfway into the canyon, she stopped to nibble on a small shrub. Somehow, Molly didn't have much of an appetite, so after a moment, she quit eating and began practicing a little melody she had made up the previous week. But now, the sound of the melody didn't please her either, so she stopped.

"Rubbish," Molly said to a nearby rock. "Its just not fair!" The rock couldn't answer, of course, which was fine with the fretful, little jackalope. She preferred talking to things that couldn't talk back and couldn't make fun of her. So it was quite a shock when a voice spoke from behind a large bush behind the rock.

"Why is everything always supposed to be fair?"

Molly drew back in sudden fright. By the movement of some leaves, she realized that someone, or something, was behind the bush. As she stared, an old jack rabbit hopped slowly out into the open. Jack rabbits and jackalopes are closely related and speak the same language.

"Molly, you have to learn to accept what life gives you."

The hair on the old one was mostly gray, and the tip of one long ear was missing.

"There is usually some good with the bad. You may have to search for the hidden treasures," he added and gave Molly a knowing look.

"Who are you? What do you know about me? I've never seen you before!" Molly had gotten over her surprise and was getting a little irritated. "My name is Grandal," was the reply. "I have watched you come into this little canyon many times and have heard you singing. I have seen you at other places too."

"That's strange," Molly said and hesitated a bit. "Well, if you've seen me before, you've probably noticed my missing antler. It makes me look like a freak. And … and, my voice sounds funny to the other jackalopes."

Grandal wiggled his ears for a moment. The one with the missing tip seemed to flop over a little, then it righted itself. A close call with a coyote in his younger days had left this mark on the old jack rabbit. He had become more cautious after that, and often sat behind rocks and bushes for long periods of time, watching and listening. Over the years, Grandal had observed many things and had become very wise.

"Well," he finally said, "you can't change your appearance. But it's not good to think very much about it. If you act as if it is not important, a surprising thing will happen. Soon, the other jackalopes will not pay much attention to the missing part and will learn to take you for who and what you are."

"They call me, "Dope-a-Long Bunny,"" and giggle when I try to sing with them." Molly was still hoping for some sympathy.

"Learn to smile and laugh when you hear that," advised Grandal. "Don't take yourself too seriously. Once the others discover that your feelings are not easily hurt, most of the teasing will stop."

The little jackalope was silent. After a pause, Grandal continued, "I have listened to your voice," he said, "and I think you have a special gift."

"How can that be? I know my voice sounds different from the others."

"Different doesn't mean it is not as good." The old jack rabbit gazed up to the small, windblown trees scattered along the rim of the canyon. "Hearing you sing reminds me of the sounds of the wind, of moving water, of distant birds speaking to each other."

"Those are the things I listen to when I am out here," replied Molly. "They give me a good feeling inside, and it just comes out in the songs I sing."

"And that is your gift!" exclaimed Grandal. "Sing what is truly in your heart, and the gift will never leave you. But to reach others, you must touch what is in their hearts, also. Go beyond yourself! When you have discovered how to do this, you will indeed find your hidden treasure." With those words and a final flop of the shortened ear in Molly's direction, the jack rabbit seemed to fade back into the brush. After a few seconds, Molly hopped behind the bush to see if Grandal was still there. But he was gone.

Moving out of the canyon, the little jackalope paused several times to browse on grass and the tender leaves of shrubs that were edible. She wanted to finish eating before starting across a small, open plain on her way home. Fortunately, there were some scattered bushes and cacti in the plain for cover. Still, it was necessary to be very careful and watch for hungry coyotes and hawks in the sky when making that dangerous crossing. It would not be a good place to stop and eat.

A couple of hawks were in the sky that afternoon, but were circling about a mile away intent on catching a large rat they had spied among the rocks. From their lofty position, Henry and his donkey, along with his grazing flock were clearly visible, and a few antelope could be seen in the distance. An occasional, small cloud drifted above, however most of the sky was clear and blue. But the hawks did not see the jackalope.

At the far edge of the open area, there was a thicket of small trees and brush. As Molly reached the thicket, she breathed a sigh of relief. Adding to her comfort was the sight of a familiar friend. This was Fraida, a large, black-and-white bird with a long tail, known as a magpie. Fraida was busy moving from bush to bush in search of seeds and insects, but paused when she saw Molly.

"*Chiga, chiga*. . . whatcha doin', Mollylope? Happy ta see ya. . . *chiga, chiga*. . . gotta catch that bug. . . gotcha! What's uh going on out there, Mollylope?" Magpies have a reputation for chattering a lot. At times, Molly thought her friend was a bit of a bore, but at this moment she was glad to see her.

"Not a lot, Fraida. But I did meet an old jack rabbit named Grandal. He surprised me, kinda. He seemed to know a lot about me."

The magpie stopped eating suddenly. "Old Grandal, eh? Verra, verra wise. . . verra wise! *Chiga, chiga.*" She cocked one eye at the jackalope. "Not many creatures get ta see Grandal. Guess you're one of the lucky ones, *chiga, chiga.*"

"Why don't the others see him, Fraida?"

"*Chiga, chiga*, don't know, Mollylope. He said something one time about 'Merlin's ring,' *chiga, chiga.* Don't know what that has to do with it." Fraida shook her feathers and looked up at the sky.

"Gotta watch for any hawks. They wanna getcha! But, *chiga, chiga*, they won't get me, *chiga, chiga.*" With that, she flew to another bush and busied herself looking for more insects.

Molly said good-bye to the magpie. Hopping away, her thoughts returned to her conversation with Grandal and the things he had said. Perhaps the old jack rabbit was right; she did spend a lot of time feeling sorry for herself. But what could she do to change the way the other young jackalopes treated her? Grandal seemed to be saying that it was all up to her.

The western sun was settling low in the sky when Molly reached the village where the jackalopes lived. As she made her way around some rocks and shrubs, two of her cousins saw her approach and one of them called to her.

"Hey, Dope-a-Long! Look where you are going! Are you sure you aren't moving sideways?"

"Yeah," giggled the other one, "better watch out for that tree over there!"

Now normally, little Molly would have turned away from the others when they said these things to her. Feeling hurt and angry, she would have hurried to her burrow or to some place where she could be alone again. But this time, she stopped for a moment, then surprising herself, hopped over to where the two jackalopes stood.

"I guess I do look a little funny, moving along the way I do." She looked at one, then the other.

"Can't blame you for laughing. . . anyway, thanks for telling me about the tree." Molly smiled at them and hopped away slowly.

The two jackalopes sat quite still for a moment. This was a different Molly than the one they remembered. Glancing somewhat sheepishly at each other, they went over to a group of other young jackalopes playing a game called "Ring-a-Round-the-Cactus."

Molly didn't pause to watch the others in their play as she sometimes did from some hidden spot, out of their view. The evening air was getting cool, the sun was almost down and she was having a strange feeling about the night that was coming. Something inside was telling her she had to be somewhere else that night. But where? And why?

Then suddenly, she remembered the old sheepherder, and the sound of his flute. Henry's camp was almost two miles away. Quite possibly he and his animals had already left the area. But the voice inside Molly grew louder. She must go tonight! She had learned from experience to obey that little voice when it spoke to her. But still, she was a little fearful and uncertain about what might happen. So, as the long evening shadows faded slowly into darkness, the little jackalope, with only one antler, began her journey back to the sheepherder's camp near the rocky ridge.

When Molly hopped off into the darkness, she could hear the voices of the other jackalopes as they practiced little snippets of songs and tunes they would sing near some cowboy's campfire that night. This time, however, she didn't feel the hurt and disappointment at being left behind by the others. In fact, she was somewhat proud of being out on her own mission even though it wasn't clear what she was going to do.

After picking her way through scattered scrub bushes and cacti for a half mile, the jackalope decided to try and take a shortcut. She turned a little and started across a small, low ridge with an outcropping of rocks. A pale moon had just risen in the eastern sky. By the moon's dim light and the light from numerous stars, Molly could make out the outline of several large rocks up in front of her. Starting to go around the edge of these, she was suddenly startled by a quiet voice.

"Be careful in this place, Molly!" And old Grandal moved out of one of the shadows.

"There is a den of rattlesnakes here in these rocks, and the larger ones are out looking for food just now. It's best that you move down below the rocks."

To himself, Grandal muttered something sounding like "children of Mordred," which made no sense at all to Molly, but she shivered. Certainly, she didn't want to stumble onto a big rattlesnake there in the dark. She felt grateful to the old jack rabbit, and they both hopped a little distance away from the rocks. Then with great curiosity, Molly asked, "How did you happen to be here?"

"I've been following you," replied Grandal, "and I think I know where you are going."

"But how could you know that? I didn't even tell any of the other jackalopes. . . anyway, they would have said that I was quite foolish." At that moment, Molly was feeling a little bit foolish herself and wondered why she had come.

"No, you are not being foolish, Molly," said the old one. In the moonlight, she could see the tip of Grandal's ear bend slightly in her direction as it had before.

"This is a special night," he said. "It is a night for living your dreams and doing great things." He stopped and straightened his ears to listen to the sounds of the desert night. A lizard scurried by into a small crevice. Faintly, from the distance came the hooting of an owl. An occasional breeze moved a nearby tumbleweed.

Molly listened, too, particularly for any sounds that might be from coyotes. Finally, she spoke in a low voice.

"The man that was there with the sheep. He played the flute, and it's voice seemed to speak to me. He seemed so alone and. . . sad and. . . ." It was hard for her to finish the sentence.

"He is still there, and he seems to carry a heavy burden in his heart." Grandal had watched Henry with his animals for a long time and knew about Sorene. "I know a few things, but I don't know all of the reasons for his sadness."

"Why does he stay there so long?" Molly wondered aloud. "The sheep must have eaten most of the grass by this time."

"I'm not certain, but I think he is waiting there for something to happen."

"But for what, Grandal?"

"Perhaps for something new and different. He probably doesn't know himself just why he is waiting. Maybe it will be something that will give him hope, something that he can't do or find all by himself." Grandal gazed at the little jackalope for a moment. "Molly, this may be why a voice is telling you to go there tonight."

All of this was very mysterious to Molly. Yet, she had known somehow that this trip tonight would be special. But there was so much that she did not understand. She could not think of how to answer Grandal, and so she was silent.

"It's time that you should be going now, Molly," the old one urged. "I am not just sure what you will be called to do. But, whatever it is, remember to look deeply into your own heart and do what it tells you. And use the great gift that you have!"

Before Molly could reply, Grandal's form seemed to drift away a few feet and melt into the shadows. Again, he was gone.

An hour later, Molly slipped silently into the underbrush near Henry's camp. From her position, she could watch the campfire and also hear the occasional movements of the sheep. Everything seemed peaceful. But Molly was worried. About a half mile back, before she had reached the camp, she had first heard, then saw, the forms of several coyotes as they crossed a little distance in front of her. Freezing in one spot for a long moment after the coyotes had gone, the little jackalope had been stricken with fear. It was only with great effort that she found the courage to go on.

With the coyote pack this close, there was a real danger they would find and attack the sheep before morning. Molly herself could be caught and eaten by one of the hungry creatures. She was now very uneasy as she hid in the brush and gazed at the flickering flames of the campfire. As the moments passed, the sight of the fire itself seemed somewhat comforting. Molly's heartbeat slowed back to its normal rhythm. Perhaps the coyotes wouldn't come at all.

Henry emerged from a small hut he had built and came over to the fire. The sheepherder looked even older than before. His pace was slower. More wood was needed for the fire, and he took his time bringing several sticks from a little pile near the small stream. After building up the fire again, Henry sat for a little while, apparently deep in thought. But a wave of restlessness seemed to come over him, and he got up and walked to the edge of the lighted

area. There, he gazed in the direction of the flock of sheep, which was bedded down for the night.

There was reason for Henry's unrest. During the afternoon, he had taken a walk some distance away from the campsite and had seen fresh coyote tracks. He knew these animals couldn't be far away. Certainly tomorrow, he and his flock must leave this place and move southward where they would be safer. Perhaps he had already tarried too long. Now it was dark again; his fear rose as he strained his eyes to look into the shadows beyond the firelight. The night was threatening, and he would try to keep watch as long as possible It would be good if he could find something to do that would keep him awake.

Molly watched the old sheepherder as he stood gazing out into the shadows. She continued to watch as he finally turned, but instead of walking back to the fire, he went over to the hut. From there, he returned in a short time, carrying his flute.

Henry's first notes moved him into an old, slow melody that he had learned as a boy, the notes coming out clearly as memory carried him back. Then he attempted to move into something more lively, but somehow his heart was not in the effort. The flute's voice seemed to falter, almost stopping, then stumbling on through a few more notes before it stopped. After several seconds of silence, there came one more note from the flute—long and sorrowful, quivering on the night air.

Suddenly, another sound began to be heard. It was the voice of someone singing, very low at first, then rising in volume, the notes coming sweet and clear with a wondrous range in pitch and tenor. Molly, the little jackalope, had listened to the faltering notes from the flute, then scarcely realizing what she was doing, began to speak back to it. Oh, she wanted the flute and its player to know what she felt at times, to hear about the music from the waters of the brook, about the joyous calls of birds and the melodies sung by the winds and rain. Her heart wanted to speak about sorrow, about clouds and sunshine, and about the colors in a desert sunset. So, Molly sang!

The flute player sat mute for a long moment, scarcely believing the magic that his old ears were hearing. The sound seemed to be everywhere. Then his flute rose to his lips again, almost of its own accord it seemed, and he began to respond to the voice, slowly at first, and finally in full symphony. On and on they continued in perfect harmony, both lost together in a musical world of their own. Neither Henry nor Molly was completely conscious and thinking at that time. It was as if something within each of them had to find its way out, and the only path was through the music.

The sheep had stopped their murmuring and were perfectly still. On a small hill in the distance, the pack of coyotes had lifted their ears when they heard the first notes of the flute. Their curiosity was fully aroused this time. They began to move quickly in the direction of the sound and toward the

tiny light they could see in the distance. Then, the jackalope's voice rose into the air, and it and the flute came together as one. The coyotes stopped as if halted by some invisible force. They sat on the hillside and began to howl in concert. A large hunting owl, flying low and soundlessly over the desert, saw a prairie dog sitting out in the open, but strangely the owl flew on, sparing the little animal.

Above all, the pale moon seemed to have become a little brighter, and a thousand stars twinkled and twinkled. Finally, the melodies began to slow, and the magical spell was broken. Both the sheepherder and the little jackalope sat entranced and silent in their own places. Both were somewhat breathless and still overwhelmed by the experience. It was obvious something wonderful had occurred. Neither of them could explain it, but somehow, for that moment, it had made the world just a little bit better.

On the distant hillside, the coyotes were at first quite still. Then the leader, looking back toward the campsite once, led the pack far away in the opposite direction. The next morning, they busied themselves chasing a couple of antelopes.

On the trip back to her home that night, Molly felt tired, but unusually happy and content. She now understood more

of the meaning in Grandal's words. In this one night, she felt she had become older and wiser. Tomorrow would be a new day, and she looked forward to seeing some of the other young jackalopes. She was becoming a different Molly now, and the others would have to realize that.

Henry closed down the campsite early the next morning and started southward with his donkey and the sheep. Over the next few days, he again found joy in seeing little lambs at play, or listening to a flock of crows calling to each other, or watching a glorious sunrise over the blue, desert hills. But as he walked, again and again, Henry's mind returned to the night when that singing voice started coming from the shadows. Did it really happen? Or was it just a dream?

In time, the old sheepherder would go on to new places, and he would do some new things. But during his remaining years, he would sometimes look up at the night sky and wonder again about that mysterious time when he thought he played the flute and heard the marvelous song coming seemingly from nowhere. He was thankful because it had been a gift.

Molly and the Ginkgo Tree

Near the mouth of a small ravine not far from the jackalope village stood a lone tree. It was indeed unlike any others there for it had grown from a Ginkgo seed dropped by a bird flying many miles away from its home. The little Ginkgo tree was watered by occasional rains in the winter and spring. But being in the desert, it grew very slowly. Because it was so far from its own kind, it was often very sad.

One afternoon in the early spring, many of the desert creatures were out enjoying the freshness of the air and the warm sunshine. New green leaves were growing on many of the shrubs, and there was young, tender grass in some places. Molly Jackalope was making the most of the opportunity since the winter had been long, cold and dreary. As she nibbled on one of the shrubs, her nose seemed to wiggle with every movement of her little mouth. But while she ate, her eyes were fixed in the direction of the Ginkgo tree and the movements that were taking place in a flat area nearby the tree.

Several other jackalopes were playing "Jack Jump High," a favorite game for those that were more nimble. They would

gather in a ring with one jackalope standing in the middle. Then one of animals in the ring would lower its head with its little antlers in front and charge toward the one in the middle. As the charger came close, the middle jackalope would leap high, letting the other pass underneath. After three successful jumps, another jackalope would take the position in the center of the ring. This game would go on sometimes for an hour or more with lots of laughter and squeals of excitement. Sometimes, while the jackalopes were playing, Molly's magpie friend, Fraida, would fly in and sit on one of the Ginkgo tree branches among the fan-shaped leaves, chattering and chattering. So, when Molly observed that Fraida had arrived there on this occasion, she left the shrub and hopped over near the players' circle.

"Loooka that, *chiga, chiga!*" cried the magpie, "Watch it! *Chiga, chiga,* he'll getcha, getcha!" as a leaping jackalope barely escaped the charger's rush. Molly could not help but smile at her friend's noisy commentary.

"Hey, there, Mollylope, *chiga, chiga.* Whatcha doin'? These friends of yours gonna break their necks!" With that, the bird flew to a branch closer to the little jackalope. In a quieter tone, Fraida said, "Haven't seen you over across the prairie lately, *chiga, chiga.* You know. . . down where the sheepherder was."

For a while, Molly was silent. There had been a special enchantment about the night she sang near the sheepherder's camp. It was still difficult for her to talk about it even now, months later. Old Grandal was the only creature she knew she could share that experience with. But Molly had gone back to the little canyon and other favorite places many times since, hoping to see the phantom jack rabbit. Search as she did, there was never a trace of Grandal. Finally, she began to wonder if perhaps the whole thing had been just a dream, or a figment of her imagination.

"No, I guess it's not too safe to go over that way again." Molly wanted to change the subject. "Priscilla there," referring to a cousin of hers in the game circle, "says she saw three coyotes in that direction last week, and it was just at daybreak. They must have been hunting most of the night."

Just then, a large, heavy jackalope named Jumbo jumped into the center of the circle. In attempting to leap up over the one who was charging at him, Jumbo failed to get high enough and crashed down onto the back of the unfortunate creature, causing both to roll onto the dirt. The others laughed uproariously, while poor Jumbo grinned a sheepish jackalope grin. After righting himself, he lumbered over to a point outside of the circle. There he sat down to rest, both ears twitching nervously.

The magpie began scolding furiously, "*Ha, ha, ha!* Serves you right! *Chiga, chiga, chiga*. Too fat, too fat. . . gotta eat less. . . ," then suddenly she stopped in mid sentence. For a strange thing was happening.

The branches of the Ginkgo tree had all been leaning down somewhat in the direction of the jackalopes' game. Then suddenly, they all straightened up. The tree seemed to give itself a vigorous shake, upsetting the magpie, which flew away with a loud squawk, "*Awwwwk*! Sky's falling, sky's fallin'...," and her voice trailed off into the distance. The game below ended abruptly as the surprised jackalopes leaped hastily away from the tree. Some thought the departing bird might have seen something in the distance like an approaching coyote, and they began hurrying back to their burrows. Soon Molly, who had been observing the magpie and the tree when the disturbance began, was left alone with the Ginkgo tree whose broad leaves were again rustling gently in the breeze.

"Very strange," said Molly to herself, "I've never seen a tree do that before." She hopped over to look behind it,

thinking that maybe somebody was hiding there and had pushed on the trunk. Nope, nobody at all was in sight. Then came a whispering sound so soft that Molly first thought it must have been the wind. It came a second time from the direction of the tree itself, and Molly, listening intently, could make out the actual words, " Dear me, dear me," and the tree seemed to give a deep sigh. Startled, the little jackalope backed away.

"No, no," she heard the voice again, "don't worry. You don't have to go now. I just want to have someone to talk to." Molly's own voice shook a little when she finally replied, "I'm sorry, but you gave me such a fright. I've. . . I've never heard a tree talk before."

"We do talk sometimes," the whisper continued, "but most folks don't really hear us. They just think it is the wind blowing, or our leaves rustling. You have to be kinda special and really interested in us to be able to hear us talking."

"You seemed sad just now. Is it because you are alone out here?" Molly remembered that she had never seen another tree like the Ginkgo. How did you ever get here anyhow?"

"I don't really know," answered the tree with a little shrug of its branches, "I just remember growing up out of the ground here. It's a good thing you and your friends don't seem to like eating my leaves, or I might never have gotten past the baby stage."

Molly gave a little, rabbity chuckle, "I guess you're right. Some of the plants around here must have a really hard time with all the creatures that chew on them. Anyway, I'm glad you had a chance to grow. It's nice to have a place to sit in your shade when the sun is hot."

"It's nice for me, too. As long as the animals don't scratch my bark too much, I am glad to have the company … even though they really don't understand when I whisper to them." The tree leaned slightly in Molly's direction. "I have been watching you for a long time. You are different from the others. Sometimes, when you sat over here by yourself, you used to sing little snippets of songs, but not so loud that the others would hear you."

"That's because I was afraid they would laugh at me," and the jackalope looked a bit sheepish. "But one night out at the sheepherder's camp, I learned not to be afraid anymore. So now, I do sing with my friends sometimes." Then she added, "Even if they laugh at something I do, that doesn't bother me either. I just try to laugh along with them."

"Wonderful!" came the soft voice of the tree, "I wish I could laugh sometimes, and then the animals would know

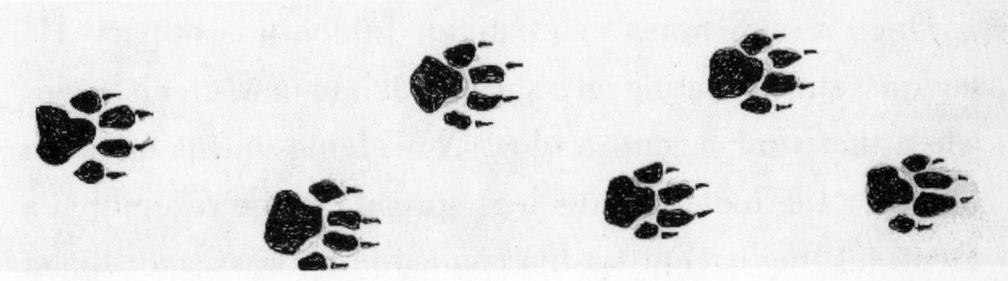

that I am laughing with them. But it is so hard just being a tree and rooted in one spot all the time. Really, there's not much for me to laugh about."

Molly felt very sorry for the tree. She could see the truth in what the tree was saying, and this made her a little depressed. In order to cheer things up a bit, she exclaimed, "Well, there is always the sunshine waiting behind every cloud! Now that we have gotten to know each other, I'll be coming back to visit with you often. But I have to go now. Good-bye!"

As Molly hopped away, she failed to hear the tree's murmuring voice, "I'm glad. It. . . it's so good to have a friend."

The next day brought wind and clouds to that part of the desert. It didn't rain, but the wind blew tumbleweeds all about, and dust swirled around in areas that were very dry. The Ginkgo tree leaned with the wind while stronger gusts caused a few leaves and twigs to separate from their branches and go dancing and twirling out across the land. A lone crow in the sky seemed to struggle with the wind, and finally changed its direction, flying much farther south than it had intended. This was a time when most desert creatures sought shelter from the weather, hiding in holes, under or behind rocks, or wherever they could find cover. Most of them were quite patient, waiting for the wind to die down.

One creature wasn't so patient. Jumbo was hungry. He had just started eating on a shrub that had new, green leaves when the wind began to blow. Now, lying on his stomach behind a big rock with his legs spread out, he resembled a great, fat frog except for his head. Jumbo was eager to get back to his breakfast, hoping that the other jackalopes wouldn't find the bush and get there first. If that did happen, he would simply push them away and position his body crosswise on one side of the plant to prevent the others from reaching it. Of course, Jumbo did believe in sharing—the others could have what was left when he had finished! So, while the hard wind blew, Jumbo was only listening to the rumble of his nearly empty stomach.

The wind blew all day and most of that night, but as the sun rose again, there was a change in the weather. A gentle, warmer wind came in from the south, and the sky cleared. Most of the creatures were out early looking for food. Molly had gone a short distance out onto the prairie, and now was slowly making her way back, nibbling on this bush and that bush. She wanted to check on her friend, the Ginkgo tree. As she moved closer, she could see several other jackalopes over near a light-green shrub. Jumbo's body was there blocking one side while his head was nearly buried among the leaves. "*He only thinks about food and himself*," thought Molly, then aloud she said, "Not much I can do about it, or anyone else." Near the ravine, the Ginkgo tree was taking stock of its limbs and branches after the windstorm.

"Well," it whispered to itself, "some leaves and twigs are missing, but otherwise, things are okay. It's good that I have strong roots." There was a dead limb on the tree to the side facing the ravine, but it was still firm and had not broken off. So the tree gave a happy little shrug, rustling its leaves.

Meanwhile, a large, brown animal was making its way up and out of the ravine beyond the tree. It was a badger, and it,

too, was hungry after the storm; yet, it had found little to satisfy its hunger. Badgers usually hunt mice, rats, lizards and prairie dogs when they can find them. Often a badger will team up with a coyote and raid a prairie dog village, the badger going down into the burrows after the little animals while the coyote waits outside. But this time, there was no prairie dog village nearby. As the badger came out to the edge of the ravine, its sharp eyes spotted the movement of the jackalopes feeding. Keeping its body close to the ground, it crept slowly toward some brush at the base of the only nearby tree that could be used for cover. One of the jackalopes in particular seemed to be making its way in the direction of the tree. With most of its body concealed, the badger's sharp eyes were fixed on the creature's approach as it hopped along casually, sometimes a bit off balance due to one missing antler.

Normally, a badger would not waste time trying to catch a jackalope or jack rabbit, which can run very fast on the open prairie. But in a small space, the badger can move quickly, and with its powerful jaws and sharp teeth, it can easily kill either of these animals. Molly and her friends knew this and usually kept a wide distance from any badgers they encountered. But this time, Molly did not see the danger that awaited her as she approached her friend. She was thinking about the Ginkgo tree's loneliness and what kind of things she could do to cheer it up.

About ten feet away, Molly suddenly was aware that something was moving behind a little bush next to the tree. . . it was the badger readying itself for the short dash and a quick struggle with the doomed jackalope. Before she could move, however, there was a sudden cracking sound together with a loud "*Thump!*" Thoroughly astonished, Molly leaped backward while a big, furry, brown animal struggled from under the dead limb that had fallen on its head. Scrambling to its feet, it rushed away down the ravine.

"That was a badger," Molly shivered with the recognition, "and it could have killed me. . . except for that limb that fell!" Still shaking, she stared at the tree. Seeing a faint rustle of the Ginkgo tree's limbs, Molly crept closer and heard its familiar whisper, "That was a close call, Molly! I barely dropped the limb on that badger in time. Are you. . . you okay?"

"You mean you did that on purpose?" the jackalope marveled. "I thought it was a freak kind of accident. . . lucky for me you did do it!"

"Sometimes I can do things like that just by thinking about it," said the tree. "I am so happy you are safe and that I could really do something to help a friend."

"You saved my life." Molly was deeply grateful and stayed with the tree for the rest of the morning, keeping it company and talking about many different things together. She was glad the other jackalopes had been frightened by the commotion with the badger so that none of them came close enough to see her talking with her leafy friend. Indeed it would have created a new rumor to the effect that the little "Dope-a-Long Bunny" had been eating the desert loco-weed and spent all morning talking to herself. So, it was well after the noon hour before she thought again about being hungry and finally departed to find something edible.

One thing that the Ginkgo tree had said remained in Molly's mind throughout the afternoon. This concerned a certain practice that many of the larger girl jackalopes had developed recently. As they became older, girl jackalopes were normally more preoccupied with how they looked. It was not enough to merely appear clean with nice, soft fur and little, polished antlers. Something extra was needed, and Molly's cousin, Priscilla, had provided this by appearing one day with a leafy sprig from the Ginkgo tree tucked among her antlers. She was a very vain creature, and she pranced about hoping to win the others' admiration. Indeed, she succeeded, and it was no time before the other girls were doing the same thing, each plucking a sprig from the tree and wearing it in her antlers.

In fact, things got to the point where most of the girls were ashamed to be seen without the now-familiar sprig of Ginkgo

leaves. Poor Molly herself had tried to imitate the others in the past, but having only one antler, she was unable to get anything to stay in place. So, sprigless, she had suffered the fate of not being able to conform, a creature to be somewhat pitied. In time, this had become less important to her, and by now, Molly found the silly habit somewhat amusing. But she had kept this to herself.

The Ginkgo tree had said, "I am so tired of having my lower branches pulled and tugged at by your little friends. Already, you see, they have pretty much stripped off all the leaves within their reach. It's a good thing my other branches are higher, or I would soon be bare and leafless." Molly could see proof of what the tree was saying with her own eyes. So the situation was troubling to her, and Molly continued to think about it as she wandered about eating what was now a very late lunch.

The next morning, Molly talked to Priscilla. Her cousin was as carefully groomed as a jackalope could be. Her hair was smoothed down, except for the tail, which was white and fluffy. The Ginkgo sprig was neatly arranged in her antlers. In addition, Molly noted that Priscilla had dipped the tips of her ears in the white, chalky dust found in some parts of the desert—giving them a powdery look. This was the most recent fashion trend, and some of the more ordinary-looking jackalopes had not yet tried it. "Have you been over to the Ginkgo tree lately?" Molly began, "I've noticed most of its leaves are gone around the lower branches."

"Well, that's too bad," and Priscilla gave her head a slight toss, "I really need to get a new sprig soon. You can see that the leaves are fading a little on the one I have. I detest wearing anything that is faded!"

"Perhaps you could find something from a different kind of tree," Molly suggested. "A sprig from a Piñon tree would look nice." She was hoping to direct her cousin's attention away from her friend, the Ginkgo.

"No, no, that won't do at all. Anything from a Piñon tree, or any other old common plants around here, would be a waste of my time. There is nothing special about those. That Ginkgo tree is the only one of its kind here. If I am going to wear anything at all, its got to be the best." Then Priscilla paused a minute while a hopeful look came into her eyes. Molly waited.

"We have just got to figure out a way to get up higher to reach that tree's other branches. And. . . and, I think I may have the answer." Pricilla glanced at Molly, then continued in a confiding manner, "We girls just need to get our boyfriends to do some work for us. We'll tell them that we all need to have a platform there under the Ginkgo tree where judges can stand when we have big jackalope games. Then, when they bring in sticks and stones and pile them up to make the platform, the girls will be able to reach more branches." She had a sly smile. "The boys will do it if they think it's for the games. They won't mind work if it involves play!"

"I'm not sure that is a good idea!" exclaimed Molly. "Snakes and things might hide inside the pile. . . and even another badger might hide there." She was reminded of her close call from the day before. But Priscilla wasn't listening. Already she was beginning to hurry away to tell her plan to the other girl jackalopes. It wasn't long before the word had spread, and Molly could see boy jackalopes hopping out to search for pieces of brush and wood. When a piece was found, two jackalopes would tug on it with their teeth and drag it to the Ginkgo tree, or one would pull while the other would push from the other side with his antlers. With larger pieces, three or four jackalopes might be needed.

Molly tried to slow things down by mentioning the snake and badger danger to some of the boys, but they all laughed at that. "Oh, we'll just check everything out before a game starts." With much bravado, one even shouted, "If a badger comes, we'll all butt him with our antlers!" The others cheered, "Yeah, yeah!"

"*Sure you will. . . just like yesterday*," thought Molly to herself. She realized, however, the others would pay no heed to her.

The work continued, although the jackalopes soon found that rocks were harder to move than they had thought they would be. They did discover that two or three of them working together could use their antlers, and by setting their feet and pushing, could move some stones that weren't too heavy. It was difficult at times, but with steady effort, the animals constructed a sizeable pile by nightfall. Another half day or so, and the project would be complete. Already, Priscilla, climbing onto the top of the soon-to-be platform, was able to reach a fresh new sprig of leaves. Separating it from the branch with her teeth, she carried it off proudly to her burrow.

Tomorrow, when the pile was complete, more girl jackalopes would be visiting the tree eager to provide themselves with a new sprig as their stylish leader had done.

With the setting sun, all of the boy jackalopes quit working and went back to their homes. Molly slowly made her way over to the tree. She could tell by the slight droop of the branches that her leafy friend was sad and discouraged. The twilight was changing to night.

"It's no use, Molly," came the familiar whisper. "I know there is nothing you can do. Those foolish girls are determined to take my twigs and leaves. Soon there will be nothing left but bare branches, and I will die here. My wood will rot, and grubs and beetles will take over. After a few months, you will probably never hear my voice again."

"No! No!" cried Molly. "There must be some way to stop them. You are now too good a friend to me! I must think … think of a way!" But, try as she may, the little jackalope could not think of anything she could do to stop the building of the mound and to protect the tree's leaves from being taken. The boy jackalopes were determined to have their fun and games, and the girls were completely caught up in trying to be stylish.

Sadly, Molly climbed up onto the unfinished pile and lay there with her head on her front paws. If nothing else, she could stay there a little while and keep her friend company.

The desert night air turned cooler, and from the distance, came the hooting of an owl. Near the pile of rock and brush, Molly heard the faint rustle of a pack rat that had already discovered the pile as a place to explore.

A nearly-full moon rose in the eastern sky, bathing the desert scene below with an almost ghostly light where objects like bushes and big rocks looked larger than they actually were. Molly shivered a little, and thought for a minute about the badger that had come up out of the nearby ravine. So, it was with a bit of shock, when she heard a voice from beside the tree.

"I thought I might find you here." Sitting up quickly, she saw it was Grandal. "Molly, you are being brave to stay out here all alone tonight after that business with the badger."

"I've been hoping and hoping to see you again," replied the jackalope with a sigh of relief, "but how did you know about the badger?"

"We see much through Avalon's mists." The old jack rabbit seemed to be almost talking to himself.

"What was that, Grandal? I don't understand."

"You'll have to excuse me, Molly. Sometimes I just mutter things that don't make much sense to others. Its because I'm an old, old rabbit."

"And a most unusual one!" Molly thought to herself, and then said aloud, "What you said is true. . . I am a little scared, but my tree friend here needs help, and I can't think of what to do."

"Well," said Grandal, and he looked quite amused. "I must say that some of your little friends are behaving in a ridiculous manner. The wearing of the Ginkgo sprigs has become a big joke to many of the other animals and birds around here. Haven't you heard the crows cawing a lot lately when they pass over this place?"

"Yes, I have," replied Molly, "but I didn't know the reason. . . so they have been laughing at us. Is that it?"

"Exactly," said Grandal, "but you don't need to tell me what the problem is right now. I know there is a danger for our friend, the Ginkgo, here." As he indicated the tree with a tipping of one of his ears, the tree murmured, "Thank you for coming, Grandal. It has been a long time. In fact, I wasn't much more than a sapling when I last saw you."

"You haven't needed me much during that time. Now, it is different." The old jack rabbit fell silent.

Although realizing that Grandal was thinking, Molly couldn't restrain her anxiety. "I tried to get them to stop today. I even told them that badgers and rattlesnakes might come and use the pile as a place to hide. But that didn't make any difference. They are all so selfish !"

"They seem that way," Grandal explained, "because they really aren't aware. You have an advantage over most of the others because you understand some things better. The sad part is that some of them will probably never learn. In this case, we have to find a different way of persuading them to leave the tree alone."

"But how?" Molly's voice and the tree's whisper came at the same time.

"Something you said earlier gives me an idea, Molly." She looked at Grandal expectantly. "I know of some friends that may be able to help out," he continued, "but you must never let the other jackalopes suspect that you know the truth."

"What is . . ." Molly began, but Grandal continued. "There will be nothing for you to really fear here under the tree, but don't be surprised if tomorrow the others become afraid. Good-bye." With this rather mysterious parting, the gray form of the jack rabbit seemed to almost glide into a nearby shadow and disappear.

By this time, Molly was familiar with the strange appearances and disappearances of Grandal. So she wasn't surprised at the nature of his departure, but she still wondered about it. What was important now was that Grandal's visit made her feel better about the threat to the Ginkgo tree. After a few more minutes, and suddenly feeling quite tired, the little jackalope bade her friend good night and hopped away to her home.

About an hour before dawn, a pair of large rat-snakes

crawled quietly out of the ravine and into the unfinished pile of wood and stones under the tree. The pack rat, frightened by their arrival, managed to scurry away just in time to escape being caught and eaten.

In the early morning, Priscilla brought a younger sister, Abigail, to the Ginkgo tree. There, she intended to help her sister find a nice, new green-sprig or stem of leaves before others could arrive. This would be Abigail's first sprig, and the young animal was almost quivering with expectation. As the two started to hop onto the pile, a black head with beady eyes appeared from behind a rock at the top. In an instant, the head was followed by a long, slithering body with a pattern of brown blotches on its skin. This was one of the rat snakes, and as it moved down toward the jackalopes, its mouth stretched open, and its body, moving quickly over some dry brush, made a rustling noise.

"*Oooh!* Horrible! Run for your life!" cried Priscilla as she stumbled over sticks and rocks and fled, leaving her younger sister behind. Abigail, however, quickly overcame her confusion and also ran.

"Rattlesnake! Rattlesnake," shouted Priscilla, and her sister picked up the refrain, "Rattlesnakes! Rattlesnakes! Lots of 'em!" Hearing the shouts, other jackalopes joined the panic, and in no time, the whole community had retreated out onto the prairie.

Finally, some of the animals stopped running and began to look back. Molly was one of them since she had only heard the shouts and didn't yet know the cause. Others that had run farther began to turn around and cautiously hop back to where the watchers were standing.

"Who saw the rattlesnakes? Where were they?" some were asking.

"It was Priscilla. I heard her shouting, and that little sister of hers, Abigail." And to Priscilla who had just come up, a voice said, "What did you see over there?" An older jackalope was speaking.

"A big rattlesnake. . . and he was right on top of the pile we made under the Ginkgo tree!" Priscilla was still shaking. "I'll never go back there. . . as long as I live."

"Somebody said there were lots of them. Did you see more than one?"

"Nooo. . . but I didn't wait around. There must have been more. Anyway, I heard Abigail say there were lots of them." Priscilla was a little impatient with the questions. Abigail's answer, when they asked her, was nothing but a little moan and, "Snakes, lots and lots of snakes."

Molly, when hearing all of this, smiled a little and thought with amusement. "*This was all of Grandal's doing. None of the others here will go near that place now.*" But she thought, too, it was strange that Grandal would send rattlesnakes to guard the tree after he had told her there would be nothing for her to fear. So later in the day, when the others weren't around, she decided to go see for herself. As Molly approached the tree, she could see two fairly-large snakes moving about. One was on the pile of brush and stones; the other was busy investigating a tiny frog over near some other rocks. She stopped about thirty feet away and looked carefully. "Those aren't rattlesnakes," she said. "I have seen them around in other places. They hunt mice and rats and other little creatures, but they won't harm me." So, Molly hopped closer.

"Did Grandal send you?" she addressed the one on the pile. It raised its head, looked at her for a moment and went, "*Shhhhhhh!*"

"That's okay, the others won't hear us," said Molly as she edged closer to the tree.

"*Shhhhhh!*" said the snake again, and it crawled down through a hole in the brush to take a nap.

So, that's the story of how the Ginkgo tree was saved. The rat snakes decided to stay there for a while since it was a good place to attract mice and rats. From the distance, the community of jackalopes could see the snakes there, but only Molly knew they weren't rattlesnakes. At times when things were quiet, Molly would visit with her friend, the Ginkgo tree, whose lower limbs soon began growing fresh, new stems and leaves.

Over behind a rock several feet away, Molly had discovered a small plant growing from one of the Ginkgo's seeds. In time, it would become a tree, and then her friend would have another of its own kind. Molly knew this, but she didn't tell the tree. She wanted it to be a surprise.

An Unlikely Rescue

Molly was having a quiet morning. For the past two hours, she had been with her old Aunt Sofie looking for the most tender leaves and blades of grass at the edge of the prairie. Aunt Sofie was partially blind, and some of her teeth were missing. It was only with assistance from a few kindhearted jackalopes like Molly that she was able to find enough food to eat. So, Molly had gone from bush to bush and from grass patch to grass patch, nibbling on the leaves first. As she discovered which ones were the most tender, she would direct Aunt Sofie to those. While the old jackalope was eating, Molly was scanning the skies and nearby terrain to make sure no hawks or coyotes were in sight. The old jackalope nosed around among the tender leaves and chewed slowly. It took her a long time to get enough for a meal.

"Molly, you are so good to come with me like this. Didn't you want to be playing with some of the others?" Aunt Sofie had lifted her head and looked generally in Molly's direction. She knew her niece was out there somewhere.

"Not really, Aunt Sofie." Molly was telling the truth when she said this. Occasionally now, she did play in some of the games, but increasingly found a lot of them rather boring. Often, she decided it was more interesting just to observe the other jackalopes in their antics, or she would take little excursions by herself to see what was happening in other places. Then today, of course, she knew that her old aunt needed her help.

"I'm glad sometimes to get out where it is quiet and watch and listen for other animals and birds. It's too bad you can't see very well, Aunt Sofie. But I'll tell you about some of the things I see now if you would like."

"Please do, Molly. I remember a few minutes ago, I heard a group of crows scolding something in the sky, but I couldn't see what it was."

"Well, they were after a hawk that was flying up over that little humpbacked ridge. Guess they didn't give him much time to look in our direction, or we would have had to hide somewhere quickly."

Aunt Sofie breathed a sigh of relief and wheezed just a little as she spoke, "That's why I'm afraid to come out here by myself anymore. If I tried to do that, the hawks or coyotes would soon be picking my old bones pretty clean."

"We surely don't want that to happen." Molly paused, then continued, "A little while ago, I could see three antelopes grazing out on the plain. Two were grown and one was young. It was fun to watch that one. It was pretty frisky." Molly gave her little rabbity chuckle.

"Antelopes are like that when they are young, jumping all about. But I'm becoming kinda tired now." Aunt Sofie felt she had eaten enough. "Guess we better go back. You lead the way, Molly."

As the two jackalopes made their way slowly (for Aunt Sofie's sake) past some cactus and several small rocks, Molly suddenly stopped and looked at something moving a short distance away.

"You wait here, Aunt Sofie. I want to check on something I see over there." She hopped off to their left, but slowed her pace and approached cautiously as she recognized the creature. Ahead of her was a very large, heavy-bodied lizard with black and yellowish bands around its blunt tail. The rest of its body seemed covered with white, yellow and pink beads, except for the black-toned head that turned toward the approaching jackalope. Two serpentine eyes stared at Molly as she prudently stopped about seven feet away.

"I've never gotten this close to one of these 'ol ring tails' before, she said to herself. *Actually, it is kind of pretty with all those colors, but I'm not getting any closer!"* Molly remembered the warnings she had heard from the older jackalopes about Gila monsters. She knew that if the creature managed to clamp its jaws on her, she would be dead from its poison in a few minutes. That was not a good thought. But Molly wanted to watch it for another minute.

The reptile stood facing the little jackalope as she continued to look at it. Its flat, forked tongue flicked out at her from time to time. Suddenly, it charged in a surprisingly rapid manner for a lumbering lizard. Molly was quicker, however, and leaped backward. It was time to retreat, she decided, and 'ol ring tail' was left standing, staring defiantly after her even as she rejoined her aunt.

"Was there something interesting over there? I couldn't see you very well, but it seems you came back faster than you went." Aunt Sofie looked at her inquiringly.

"It was just another desert lizard." Molly knew her aunt would worry if she knew about the two-foot "ring tail" she had just seen. "I knew we needed to get back home so you could rest." The old jackalope gazed at her niece briefly, but decided to say no more. It was true; she would welcome some rest.

That afternoon, Molly decided to take the remainder of the day for herself and started for the little canyon where she had been so many times before. The afternoon sun was hot, and on the way, she watched a "dust devil" whisking here and there with its little swirl of dust as it swept across the prairie like a phantom lady's broom. After a few minutes, Molly moved on, looking forward to getting out of the sun.

Reaching the canyon, she worked her way up near its head where there was a small spring of water. Gratefully, the little jackalope took several swallows of the cool liquid.

"Better drink plenty. Molly. You will be needing it tonight." It was old Grandal, having come up behind her without a trace of a sound. She remembered looking around carefully before entering the mouth of the canyon; there had not been another creature in sight.

"*Whew*, Grandal! You always startle me when you appear like that—even though I recognized your voice."

The old jack rabbit seemed to be more hurried than Molly had ever seen him. He was breathing a little faster, and there was a coating of dust on his fur.

"Molly, I've been looking for you for the last hour. I will need you to help me."

"Sure, Grandal. . . if I can." This was something new. Always in the past, Grandal had appeared when she or another friend had needed HIM. Molly tended to think of her mystical friend as being somewhat larger than life. She couldn't think of any way that she, a simple, young jackalope, could be of assistance to Grandal who seemed to be so wise and managed to do so many things.

"You said something about tonight. What is happening tonight, Grandal?"

"Molly, there is another creature that is in pain, and in a very bad situation. I have thought about it, and I'm going to need you in order to help that poor creature." Grandal was less hurried now and had resumed his usual grave tone with her.

"I'll try, but I don't know what I can do." Molly noticed that Grandal had carefully neglected to say what kind of animal it was. "What is the creature, Grandal?"

He gazed at her carefully for a few seconds before replying. "It's a coyote, Molly. He's been caught in a steel trap that some men put out near Thunder Mountain. He was there when I was over that way this morning."

"A coyote!" Molly was horrified. "Why do you want to help a coyote? As soon as he gets out of that trap, he will try to catch us and eat us!"

"Its natural for you to feel that way, Molly." Grandal looked very grave and almost sad. "Coyotes can't help being what they are; it's part of their nature. But they have some feelings, too, just like we do. I know this one is suffering from a lot of fear and pain just now."

"Well, that's just too bad; I can't feel very sorry for him when I think of all those sharp teeth and how his kind chases and makes meals of jackalopes like me. . . and jack rabbits, too, Grandal."

"I realize all of that," Grandal replied with a little sigh. He looked to the northwest in the direction of Thunder Mountain for a moment. Finally he continued speaking.

"I spent a little time pretty close to him over there in that trap. You know that coyotes speak a different language than us. But I have listened to some of it before. . . at a distance, of course, and I managed to communicate with him with just a few words."

Molly listened intently. What Grandal was saying was quite surprising. "The steel jaws of the trap are too strong for him to escape by himself, and there was nothing I could do to help him at that time. But I think tomorrow morning, men will probably come to check the trap. If they find him there alive, they will probably shoot him."

"But what can you do about that?" Molly was feeling nervous. "If you or I were there, they would probably shoot at us, too."

"Quite likely, Molly. . . if they saw us. But I have a plan. It's going to involve you going with me tonight."

"How can I possibly help you in getting that coyote out of a steel trap? We aren't strong enough to do that!" With a shudder, the jackalope went on, "I don't think I want to get that close to his teeth even if he is hurt."

"Molly, you won't have to be very close to him if we can follow my plan." There was a trace of impatience in Grandal's voice. "What you will be doing is using your voice. I'll tell you more about that when we get there."

It all still sounded very mysterious to the young jackalope. She wondered how Grandal could expect that by her saying or singing something, the trapped coyote would come free. But she had great confidence in Grandal, and actually was a little afraid to question him anymore. So, she simply replied, "Okay, Grandal, I'll go with you. But Thunder Mountain is a long way; I've never gone quite that far before."

"It is far. That is why we will need to start at midnight. I think we should be there by the time the sun comes up in the morning." Grandal looked as though he was measuring the miles in his mind. Then, he continued, "Yes, by sun up. That should give us enough time."

"I guess I need to drink more water. . . and eat some, too." Molly was thinking of the long trip ahead.

"You surely must, Molly. Get some rest. There won't be time for that after we start. We can meet at midnight under the Gingko tree. We will start from there." Before the old jack rabbit turned to go, he looked seriously at her for a moment and then said, "Molly, I cannot guarantee you there will be no danger. What you and I are going to try to do may be quite dangerous. Even on the trip there, we will need to be very careful. But I know you can be very brave when you need to be. Tonight and tomorrow we are going to need that courage. Please remember to do exactly what I tell you."

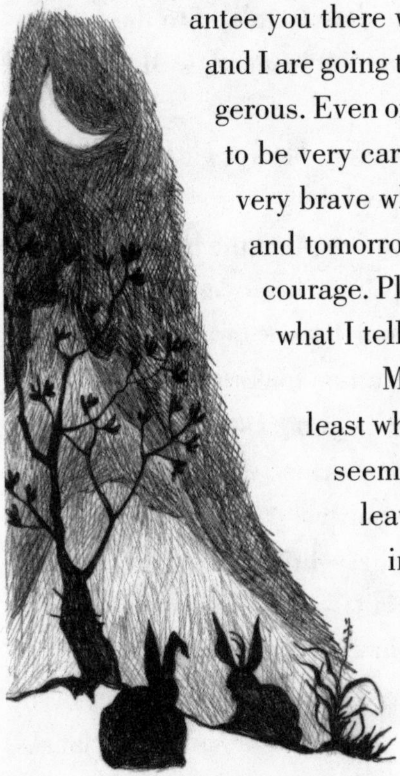

Molly wasn't surprised in the least when Grandal had finished, he seemed to fade into the brush, leaving only two small, quivering leaves on a branch.

The late afternoon brought a dark, little cloud, and it actually rained for several minutes.

The moisture seemed to clear the air, leaving a freshness and sweetness over the land. The desert plants eagerly soaked up all of the precious water they could, and the animals and birds were happy to find little pools where they could take small drinks. Molly was one of those, and by nightfall she also had eaten enough leaves and grass to feel quite full. Then she went back to her family's burrow to sleep for the first part of the night.

All of the clouds had vanished by sundown, and the coming of midnight found a star-studded sky and a quarter moon already halfway across in its nightly journey. When Molly reached the Gingko tree, she found Grandal waiting. Apparently, the old jack rabbit had already talked to the tree because its whispering voice greeted her with well wishes for their trip.

"Be careful out there tonight, Molly. I can't bear the thought of anything bad happening to you.

"I think it's going to be okay," replied the little jackalope, rubbing the last of the sleep from her eyes with her paw. "Grandal will be with me, and I have to trust him. Don't worry, we'll make it back sometime tomorrow."

"I think we should go now." Grandal's grave voice interceded. Bidding good-bye to their friend the Gingko tree, the two hopped away toward the northwest and a series of low-lying hills. The outlines of these hills were dimly visible under the starlit sky, but the dark form of Thunder Mountain lay beyond the hills, not yet in view.

Molly was familiar with the terrain for the first part of the trip, and about an hour from the start, she spotted what she

recognized as a cowboy's campfire. As the two drew closer, they heard the voices of three jackalopes singing some distance out from the fire.

"That's Priscilla and a couple of her friends," Molly observed. She always tries to make her voice sound a little better than the others."

"Like holding those high notes when it isn't necessary in the melody." Grandal almost chuckled. "In her case, it only makes her sound more artificial, Molly."

"I know," was the reply, and the two travelers detoured around the camp and continued on their journey.

They were part of the way up one of the hills and in a grove of trees when Grandal suddenly stopped and cocked his head to the side, listening. "I hear the sound of hooves."

Then, Molly could hear it, too. The scramble of hoofbeats over the rocky hillside, growing rapidly louder. In a moment, four deer, three does and a buck bounded through the patch of trees within yards of Molly and Grandal and vanished down slope in the direction of the prairie.

"Quick—over here under these rocks, Molly." The two crouched in the cover for a few minutes before Grandal decided it was safe to come out.

"You saw there were no wolves or coyotes following those deer. Something else spooked them up on the ridge there."

"What do you think it was, Grandal?"

"I'm not sure, but quite possibly it was a mountain lion. There's been one back in these hills recently. We probably should change our direction a little and go more to the north until we get around the area where those deer came from. The going may get a little rough."

It seemed that Grandal picked up the pace after that, and Molly found herself struggling and scrambling up over rocky places and down the steep sides of ravines with the gray form of the jack rabbit always up in front of her. It was almost like following a ghost, she felt, one that seemed to glide over the difficult places with no apparent effort while she even had trouble keeping her balance. Once, Molly did lose her balance and tumbled head over heels, antler and all, to the bottom of a small ravine. It was then that Grandal turned back and was at her side in an instant.

"Are you okay, Molly?" There was anxiety in his voice.

"I think so." The jackalope had gotten up and took a couple of tentative steps. "I've got some scratches and maybe a couple of bruises, but nothing serious. Let's get moving again."

Grandal led off, this time on a more even course, and Molly found it easier to follow him as the trail went down a long, gentle ridge. One leg was a little sore from the fall, but after awhile she forgot to notice it.

On the top of the next ridge was an open area among the rocks. From there, one could look down into a valley that extended to the east. A few miles up, there was what appeared to be a wooded area in the valley's center with a faint, luminous glow. As Molly stared at it, the light seemed to pulse like that from a lightening bug.

"What is that, Grandal?"

"I think you have heard its name before, Molly. That is Matamor." "So that's Matamor!" Molly shivered in spite of herself. All young jackalopes had been warned of the terrors of that place almost from the time they began to hop. By appearance, Matamor was a most delightful oasis replete with springs of water, luscious grasses and shrubs, spreading shade trees and beautiful flowers. It was said that the grass and the leaves of the shrubs that grew there were of a wonderful sweetness and tenderness, found nowhere else in the desert. A grazing animal coming close to the oasis would begin to hear the sounds of birds and feel a magnetic

attraction to the place. The closer the animal came, the greater was its desire to enter the greenness and coolness and feast on the marvelous plants.

But there was a dreadful aspect to all of this. Lurking in the shadows and behind the thick vegetation in the oasis were the very worst of predators in that part of the desert. A band of vicious coyotes, several wolves outcast from their own packs, badgers, rattlesnakes—all of these found the oasis an easy hunting ground for other unwary creatures that entered there. In fact, over the years, many had entered, but few of those ever came out. Matamor kept its own secrets, not the least of which was its mysterious pull on animals like deer, jack rabbits, antelopes, jackalopes and prairie dogs. Though the sounds of birds singing were heard, no one ever reported seeing a bird there.

Molly had heard enough to know that Matamor was a place of entrapment for any jackalope. As she stared at the pulsing light through several miles of desert night air, she realized she felt a vague but definite attraction to it. It was as if a giant magnet was trying to draw her in.

"Remind me to never get too close to that place, Grandal. I know of more than one relative that went in there and never came back."

"It would be well for you to always remember that, Molly. There is a strangeness about Matamor that I don't fully understand myself." Grandal was solemn. His eyes also seemed riveted to the phenomenon of the mysterious light. "There is a danger for me there, too, and I take great care to avoid it."

"I wonder how it ever got there in the first place." Molly's eyes were still glued in the direction of the light.

"Nobody knows," Grandal answered quietly, "it just appeared like that many years ago. An evil work indeed, it was. I've wondered about Morgan le Fey. . . ."

As Grandal's voice trailed off, Molly barely heard the last words, but they made no sense to her. Pulling his eyes away almost reluctantly, the jack rabbit turned and started to move down the ridge. Looking back, he saw his little companion still standing at the top of the ridge fixed in her fascination with what she was seeing.

"Enough now, Molly! There is no time to lose. It will be sun-up in about three hours."

The two descended the ridge and moved on past shadowy cactus in the starlight, through patches of scrub, around rocky places and past occasional trees dwarfed by the desert climate. The forms of the trees loomed like small specters in the night. Once Grandal stopped and motioned quickly to Molly with his head, and they took shelter under a large shrub. A few seconds later the outline of a large owl passed close overhead; it was so close that they felt the stir of air from its movement. Its approach had been completely silent. Molly shivered. After the sudden shock at having come so close to death, she was again left in a state of wonder. How could the old jack rabbit have possibly known the owl was coming? She had heard nothing. But she didn't think she should ask him, and they moved on.

About an hour before dawn, they paused at the edge of another ravine that extended back between two steep, little hills. A silence had settled over the land as if all of the night creatures were resting quietly in their lairs, and the day creatures weren't stirring yet. A very dim glow of light was just beginning to show in the east. By now, Molly was feeling a growing weariness.

"We'll go around this ravine to the right," Grandal directed.

"Once we get over the hill there, it is only a short distance to the foot of the mountain."

Molly didn't reply, saving her energy for the trudging climb up the hill. All night she had been wondering about the difficult trip they were making simply to help a coyote. How could any good ever come to the whole jackalope race by rescuing such a savage enemy? She felt that if the trapped coyote did get free from the trap, it would start hunting jackalopes again as soon as it was able. But Grandal seemed to think differently. Molly had put her trust in the old jack rabbit even though she had frequent doubts about the outcome. But now, having come so far, there was little she could do but keep moving until they reached their destination.

As the two gained the top of the hill, the predawn light was making it easier to see things. In front of them was the base of Thunder Mountain. The mountain itself rose majestically to a high, rocky peak well above the trees that grew

farther down on its sides. Near the top was a wide, cave-like opening among the rocks that from a distance resembled an eye. It's certainly an evil-looking eye Molly decided. At the bottom of the mountain, they could see the beginning of a small hollow between two groves of oak and pine trees. Grandal nodded in that direction, and his notched ear seemed to actually point a little bit.

"That's where I found the coyote in the trap. I think we can be over there in the next half hour. That should be well before any men come."

"I'm glad it's not much farther." Molly's voice sounded somewhat weak and strained. "But, Grandal, I still don't know what you want me to do when we get there."

"Okay, we'll rest a few minutes here while I tell you." Grandal turned and looked kindly at the weary, little jackalope.

"I know that you jackalopes can do a lot of tricks with your voices beside sing. Do you think you can sound just like a child. . . laughing or crying? How about a woman's voice?"

"Yes. I can do both of those. But how is that going to help get the coyote out of the trap?"

"Patience, Molly, I am going to explain all of that. Now, here is my plan." Grandal outlined the whole scheme to her step by step.

A short time later, the old, gray jack rabbit and his young companion approached the mouth of the little hollow they had seen earlier. A small stream with a trickle of water was flowing out from the hollow in their direction. The two stopped, grateful for a drink before continuing on. A golden ball of sun was just thrusting itself up over the eastern

horizon. Looking toward the hollow, Molly could see a humped, gray object on the ground under one of the trees. As they drew closer, she realized it was the coyote when it stood up shakily and stared at them. Its right front leg was held firmly in the steel jaws of a large trap. Molly could see dried blood crusted around that part of the leg where the skin had been torn by the animal's frantic efforts to free itself.

"Wait here," Grandal said, and then he hopped alone to within a few feet of the trapped animal. Molly watched in fearful fascination. What had started as a low growl from the coyote when Grandal first approached, changed to a pitiful little whine. Then she saw the coyote lie back on the ground with its chin resting over its left paw. Its eyes were fixed on the old jack rabbit.

"*Uhnrrrrr, mmmm, uhnrrr, ouhhh. . . .*" Grandal was making a number of strange dog-sounding noises. These he continued for about a minute interrupted only by occasional little yelps as the coyote lifted its head and stirred restlessly before again giving its attention to Grandal's voice. Finally the sounds stopped, and Grandal looked around at Molly.

"Come up closer, Molly. I want him to get a good look at you so he will recognize you again."

Molly approached in hesitant, little steps. She stared at the yellow eyes, which were now glazed with pain, and at the long, narrow jaw with its sharp teeth. Those were the eyes and teeth of a ruthless hunter and killer, she realized. Molly fought back an impulse to flee.

"I. . . I can't try to talk with him like you. . . you were doing, Grandal." Her voice seemed to come out in a series of squeaks.

"That's okay, Molly, you won't need to. I'm not sure how much he understood of what I was trying to say." Grandal looked concerned.

"All we can do now is try to carry out our part of the plan. The other part will be up to him."

Just as he spoke, there came the sound of a horse whinnying only a short distance away. Because of the trees, the source of the sound was not visible yet.

"That will be the men with their horses coming to check on the traps. Hurry, Molly, move up the creek and hide yourself behind those rocks!"

While the little jackalope hastened to obey, Grandal quickly hopped off in a different direction. Within a couple of minutes, two men on horseback came into view. They rode slowly, scanning the terrain around them, taking care to omit no detail that would be of interest to a hunter or trapper. Each carried a rifle in a scabbard next to his saddle with a rolled up poncho behind. One also had three steel traps tied behind his saddle. They were lean men with sharp eyes and weather-beaten faces.

"There it is, Jake. I believe we got us a critter!" The speaker was pointing to a spot up near the opening of the hollow. A gray form lay there on the ground. As the men rode closer, they recognized it as the body of a coyote. The ground around it had been clawed and dug into, apparently in the animal's desperate attempt to free itself from the steel jaws of the trap. Now, it lay apparently lifeless, stiff and unmoving.

"This is gonna make the second one this week." As he spoke, the man called Jake swung himself from his saddle and took his rifle from its holder. "Just wanna make sure he's dead." He walked over to the body of the coyote and prodded it with his gun barrel, first on one side, then on the other.

"Yep, Jake, 'pears to me like that one's dead alright." The other man got down from his horse. "I swear, you're gittin' as skittish as an ol' maid."

"Well, you can't be too careful sometimes."

Jake stood his rifle against a tree, squatted down and rubbed his hand over the animal's fur. "Got a real good pelt on 'im. Not all mangy like some of 'em. Here, you open up that trap, an' I'll tie 'im up behind my saddle. Like to skin 'im when we git back."

Within seconds, the body of the coyote was pulled free from the open jaws of the trap, which was reset and concealed under some leaves. New bait was put out.

"If you gonna carry that varmint back like you say, better wrap 'im in yore poncho so's not to spook the hosses." The other man walked back to his own horse.

"Guess yore right." Jake went to his horse and started to untie the poncho. Suddenly, he stopped. A little girl's voice came clearly from the hollow just above them. She seemed to be crying and fretting. The sound stopped for a few seconds, then started again. Then came a loud "*hallooo!*" in a young woman's voice. It was repeated a couple of times as the echoes reverberated from the rocks above. Jake and his partner looked at each other in amazement.

"Wal, I'll be danged. Sounds like a leedle gal an' her mommy up thar. Must be they're lost or sumpin', Jake."

"That's hard to figgur. How the heck could any womenfolk ever get out here by themselves?" Jake looked dubious. The woman's voice came again, coaxing and consoling as the child began to fret again.

"That's it! Come on, Jake. We gotta git up thar and help them folks." With that, both men started running quickly through the trees. But as they were moving, Jake remembered something.

"Mebbe I better run back an' git my rifle."

"Ain't no use to worry 'bout that. We won't need no rifle just to find those females. Come on!" The two continued on in the direction of the voices. Once into the hollow, they began to clamber around boulders and over fallen trees while the voices of the woman and the child seemed to be moving farther away. The woman seemed to be singing to the child.

"Dang it, Jake, they're gittin' more lost than ever." Jake's partner stopped and cupping both hands to his mouth, "*halloo'ed*" three times. With that, came an answering "'*halloo*" from the woman up above, and the child's voice broke into delighted laughter.

"Well, they know we're a comin' now. Shore bet that leedle gal gonna be glad ta see us in a couple of minutes. An' her momma, too!" Jake scurried ahead of his partner as both quickened their paces.

Two minutes later, Molly Jackalope hopped back into the little clearing where the coyote trap was. The body of the coyote was nowhere to be found. Grandal appeared after another minute or so with a satisfied look on his face.

"Well, that worked out beautifully! Our coyote friend here followed me up to a cave I had found before. He is limping pretty badly, but he can stay there until his leg heals."

Molly was quite anxious. "We'd better go, Grandal. Those men will be back down here when they get tired of searching up in those rocks and trees."

"You're right." Grandal looked around. The two horses, startled when the "dead" coyote suddenly awakened, had run off a short distance and were now grazing on some clumps of grass. Jake's rifle was still leaning against a tree, and a few feet away, the chain connected to the trap was visible at the end where it looped around the base of a large bush.

"There's something else I want to do first. I need you to help me. But we have to hurry!" The old jack rabbit hopped over to the rifle, and with his shoulder, bumped it so that it fell to the ground.

"Now, quick, let's get hold of the wooden part with our teeth." By doing so, the two animals managed to drag the weapon about fifty feet to a small pool located up the creek. With a little maneuvering, they got it into the center of the pool and left it there under twelve inches of water. Because of the clearness of the mountain stream, the rifle was still quite visible to anyone looking for it.

"Help me find a large stick that we can drag over to that trap." Molly located one, and in another minute, she had helped Grandal move it to the spot where the leaves concealed the deadly, steel jaws. They pushed the small end of the stick into the center of the trap. "*Snap,*" and the trap firmly held its new victim, a three-foot length of genuine, mountain-oak wood.

"Now, let's get out of here, Molly. We can talk more after a bit. We need to put some distance between ourselves and this place." With those words, Grandal broke into a run in a direction opposite from which the men had come earlier. Molly followed close behind him.

The two traveled at least a mile before Grandal decided to stop on the side of one of the small ridges they had crossed the night before. From there, the looming mass of Thunder Mountain was not visible. Molly was breathing hard, and her sides were heaving. All of the events, the exertions and the excitement of the past several hours, were taking a toll on the little jackalope. She was hoping for some rest. She was also hungry. Several edible-looking shrubs nearby looked very inviting.

"I think we can relax here for a while, Molly. It's a long trip back to your home. We need to rest first and eat something before going any farther."

Molly looked at her companion closely to see if he showed any signs of the fatigue that she felt. He was breathing a little faster than normal. The ear with the notch seemed to droop a little more. . . or so she thought. She really wasn't sure. Anyway, it was good to just sit and relax for a few minutes. Once they had caught their breath, the two of them began to nibble on the surrounding shrubs.

The morning sun was now sending its bright rays down onto the desert. The soil, the rocks, the plants and the creatures, all were absorbing the warmth, which was very pleasant after the night's coolness. Molly stretched herself out on her stomach and gazed at the trees on the top of a nearby hill. Perhaps Grandal was ready to talk now. He was still eating, but only quite casually.

"Did that coyote have any kind of name, Grandal?"

"I'm not really sure whether he did have in coyote language." He tasted a leaf from a reddish-looking plant and wrinkled his nose. "But I think we should call him, 'Traynor.'" Molly almost giggled, but caught herself. *Grandal thought of the quaintest things sometimes. 'Traynor'. . . well, why not? A name was a name,* she decided. Aloud, she continued with another question.

"How long is he going to stay in that cave?"

"Oh, most likely for at least a week, perhaps more, Molly. His leg is pretty badly injured. I made sure there were plenty of rats and mice around when I picked out the spot. He can catch those for food, and the creek is nearby for water."

The jackalope thought about the future when the coyote would be out hunting again.

"Well, I just hope he remembers that we helped him the next time he comes close to any of our own folks. To tell you the truth Grandal, I still haven't forgotten that he is one of the enemy." The old jack rabbit sighed and nibbled on the reddish leaves for another minute. Then he turned and looked into Molly's eyes.

"Sometimes you have to do what your heart tells you is the right thing to do even when there is danger. Molly, I believe something good will always come from our doing good. In some way, somehow, in some form, good will come from good."

"But how will we know, Grandal? Are you telling me that coyote is going to find good things to do for us?" Molly wasn't sure what she could believe at this point.

"No, I can't promise you that. We can only hope he might do something like that. But I do think he will remember this day for a long time. We will see. We will see." Then Grandal fell into silence. After another hour, the two felt rested and refreshed enough to continue their journey.

This time, they took no shortcuts over the rugged and difficult terrain. The old jack rabbit and the jackalope hopped along, taking their time, resting occasionally and observing things around them. Surprisingly, Molly found that the soreness from her fall the night before was gone, and she wasn't getting fatigued again. It was a glorious day in the desert; she had never seen the sky so blue nor the few clouds so fleecy and white. It appeared that even the crows were more friendly with their cawing. Once when she looked back, she could see the top of old Thunder Mountain beyond the hills behind them. In the distance, it didn't look threatening at all. In fact, it almost seemed that the "eye-shaped" opening near its top winked at her. She thought it looked like a kindly wink.

The Crippled Coyote

A pair of rock wrens flew out of the small juniper tree. They had been startled by a large, black-and-white magpie that sailed in and settled on one of the lower branches without even a "howdy do." Fraida was feeling a little cross. She had just come from visiting the cowboys' camp about three miles to the west. On past occasions, she had always been welcome there, perching on the backs of cows and picking off bugs and ticks with her beak. The cowboys felt that this was good for the cattle, and the animals themselves didn't seem to mind. It was easy eating for the magpie. But a pair of strange magpies had shown up at the camp that morning and staked out the territory for themselves. With flapping wings and loud cries, they had both darted at poor Fraida until she flew away in defeat.

So now, Fraida sat on the branch chattering away even though there was no one nearby to listen.

"*Chiga, chiga, chiga*, not fair, not fair! I got there first, *chiga, chiga*. Those were my cows, *chiga, chiga*. Bad birds, audacious and awful, *chiga, chiga*. . . ." On she went with her complaint until finally she ruffed up her feathers and shook herself. Then, the agitated bird turned around on the limb, the long, black feathers of her tail brushing against the juniper needles as she did so. The tree where she was perched was on the slope of a small ridge just above the jackalope village. After she turned, Fraida could see several jackalopes feeding on patches of grass and shrubs a short distance away. Molly was one of these. The closest one, however, was the rotund Jumbo, who seemed to be moving in Fraida's direction. Choosing a large shrub within thirty feet of the juniper tree, the big jackalope started eating. When two younger and smaller jackalopes approached the same shrub, Jumbo bullied them away.

"Gotcha this time! *Chiga, chiga.* Big bully. . . getting too fat. Too fat, *chiga, chiga.*" Fraida swooped down from her limb and flew in a circle over the jackalope's head, chattering furiously. The unperturbed Jumbo went right on eating. The magpie rarely lost an opportunity to scold and upbraid the greedy jackalope, but that didn't interfere with his meal.

"Hey! What's happening here?" Molly hopped over to investigate the cause of the fuss.

"What's up? What's a happenin' indeed,

Mollylope! *Chiga, chiga*, can't cha see? Jumbo's a bully, eatin' too much, *chiga, chiga*."

Jumbo glanced at Molly in between bites and mumbled, "That old bird, she's always loud and very nosy. Get her away from me!" He turned back to the shrub.

"Fraida, I don't think you are helping matters much." Molly hopped over under the tree where her exasperated friend had settled back on her branch. She lowered her voice. "He wants to eat all of the time. I don't know how we can change that. He won't listen to whatever the rest of us say." The magpie shifted her position on the branch and cocked her head. Jumbo had wandered farther away.

"*Chiga, chiga*, he better watch it, getting' too fat, *chiga, chiga*. Can't run fast, and a coyote's gonna get 'im, gonna get 'im!"

The mention of coyotes stirred a recent memory in Molly. It had now been two months since she went with Grandal to rescue a trapped coyote at the foot of Thunder Mountain. She supposed that the animal had recovered from its injury and was probably out hunting with other coyotes by now. But Fraida was still talking.

"Some around, *chiga, chiga*, some around. Coyotes, I mean, Molly. Gotta be careful, *chiga, chiga*."

"Are you sure, Fraida? We haven't seen any close to this place in quite awhile," Molly exclaimed.

"Saw one, *chiga, chiga*. Musta been yesterday, standin' on a hill and lookin' this way, *chiga, chiga, chiga*."

"Thank you for telling me." Molly could not repress feeling a bit alarmed. "I guess I should warn the others. But

most of them won't pay much attention. They can run faster than I can. . . except the little ones, and maybe Jumbo."

Her magpie friend had already turned her attention to the tree and the prospect of finding bugs and beetles that might have taken up residence among its branches and tiny cones. Molly said good-bye and hopped off to tell the other jackalopes about the coyote anyway. "*It would be good,*" she thought, "*if everybody would just be alert and watchful. Then, no one would likely be taken by surprise.*"

A couple of more days passed. Autumn weather had already come to the desert. The nights were chilly again, and in the daytime, Molly occasionally saw flocks of blackbirds and Canada geese winging their way south. She enjoyed the sounds of the geese as they seemed to talk to each other in the wild freedom of the sky.

One day she found another little canyon that she liked not far from the old one. Its walls were steeper than in the first one, but it seemed like a quiet, comfortable place and suitable for a little singing practice. So this morning, Molly headed for her new hideaway. Reaching it, she crossed paths with a young jack rabbit that was leaving the canyon. They nodded briefly to each other and exchanged "hellos." Molly thought of her guardian friend, Grandal, and realized she had not seen him for a while. "*One never knows*," she thought to herself, "*Grandal is like a 'will o the wisp.' He flits here and there, appearing and disappearing without warning. He'll probably show up when he wants to.*"

Inside the little canyon, the jackalope gazed for a moment at the layers of rock on the nearly-vertical walls. It would be a good place to hide she decided. Several scrub-oak trees had acorns among their leaves that were now turning yellow, and she noticed a couple of pack rats busy on the ground with the acorns that had already fallen.

"Better not let the rat snakes find you," she said in a friendly manner. The two rats ignored her and continued to pick up acorns and carry them away to a hole in the rocks.

"Well, I'm here. Now, let's see what I can practice on." Molly addressed her words to no one in particular. After looking around to make sure she was alone, she began to sing. . . first one melody, then another. At first her voice was low, but soon the volume increased until the whole canyon seemed to be filled with her musical sound. The echoes returning from the rock walls were pleasing to the singer, and she switched melodies from time to time, delighting in the sound effects she was getting. So engrossed was Molly in her musical experiments, she failed to notice at first that another voice had begun to accompany her own. Then hearing it, she stopped singing, but the other sound stopped, too. Then it came again, clear and unmistakable, and horrifying to the ears of the little jackalope. There was no question, it was the howl of a coyote (perhaps more than one), and it seemed to be coming from the direction of the canyon entrance.

Molly froze. She was petrified with fear. Her ears were on high alert, listening for the slightest sounds of anything approaching from the direction of the entrance. In desperation, she looked around for some possible avenue for escape. But her location was near the canyon's dead end; the walls were too steep for her to climb, there was no other way out but at the entrance. And there was no cave or hole large enough for her to climb into, only a few scattered rocks. She quickly took shelter behind the largest of these and crouched down. It would be a temporary shelter at best, once the coyote or coyotes entered the canyon and began searching for her. When that happened, she would be trapped with little hope for escape. In her mind, she could again see the gleaming yellow eyes of the coyote in the trap that time, and its long jaws filled with sharp teeth. Teeth like that would make short work of her, she knew.

The howl from the coyote came again, searching and melancholy. Molly crouched lower behind the rock.

"*It's waiting for me to come out*," she whispered to herself. "*It probably hopes to catch me right at the entrance before I have a chance to run into the open.*"

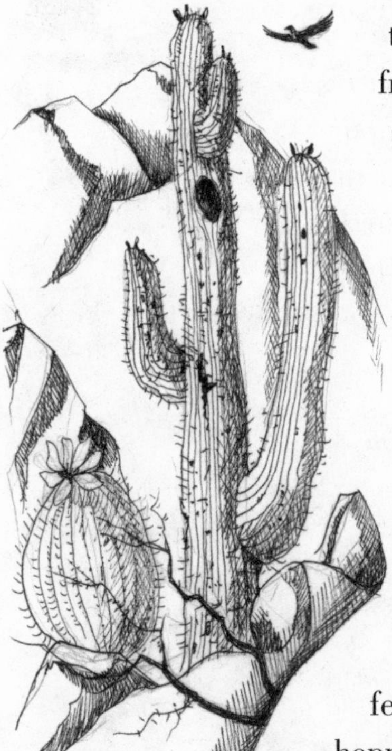

The jackalope waited a long time. Hearing no further sounds from the outside, she dared to slip back to the opening of the canyon. From there, the brightness of the noonday sun revealed nothing in sight but desert, cactus and scrub brush with rocks on the side of a nearby hill. No coyote or coyotes could be seen. With a visible sigh of relief, Molly started for home. The landscape outside seemed warm and friendly, but she still felt a slight chill inside as she hopped along. A small, gray lizard scurried out of her path, and high overhead she could see a lone vulture circling. Her route took her around the far end of the hill.

Just before coming to a point from which the jackalope village was visible in the distance, Molly happened to glance up on the hillside to her right. There, sitting out on a rocky ledge, was a coyote that was watching her. Quickly, she darted for the nearest bush. From there she broke into a full run, following a zig-zag pattern, trying to keep rocks and bushes between herself and the place where she had seen the coyote. Once she looked back, but could see nothing following in pursuit. Nonetheless, Molly was thoroughly frightened and hurried for her home. Once snug in her family's burrow, she knew she would be safe. As she ran, the magpie's warning came back to her.

"*So, Fraida was right!*" the jackalope said to herself. "*The coyotes are getting closer to us.*"

Reaching her home ground, Molly rushed close by the Ginkgo tree, but failed to hear it whisper as she passed.

"What's the rush, Molly? I don't see anything behind you."

The other jackalopes had retired to their own burrows for a noonday rest, and Molly wasted no time in seeking out her own burrow. Once there, she told her family about the coyote she had seen, but did not mention her experience in the canyon.

It was late in the afternoon before Molly emerged from her burrow to browse for the evening meal. Most of the other jackalopes were out eating. She looked very carefully in the direction of the rocky ledge where the coyote had been sitting that morning. In the distance could be seen the figures of two antelopes moving, but that was all. The scene was quite tranquil and restful. She moved to the edge of the prairie where a group of younger jackalopes were mixing play with their supper. Over to one side, her cousin Priscilla looked up as Molly approached, then sniffed and turned her head

back to eating. Priscilla disdained the playfulness of the youngsters, considering such antics as being below her dignity. Her younger sister Abigail was over near the base of the ridge talking with Jumbo, who appeared to be actually taking a short break from food. Molly chuckled and said to herself, "*Big Jumbo's found himself a favorite, now. And that silly Abigail just loves it.*"

Everybody had noticed that Jumbo was allowing the young, girl jackalope to eat with him from the most tender leaves and grasses while he pushed others away. Abigail was flattered by the special attention she was getting and often followed Jumbo around. She would wait for him to move others away from the choice eating places before she began her meals.

Molly ate awhile, and even romped with a couple of the younger ones for a few minutes. It was good to be doing something that was gay and carefree, remote from the fears that she had felt earlier. Finally, as the western sun sank into a purplish horizon of hills and cloud, the jackalope community began to drift back to its network of burrows and nesting sites. The twilight air was cooling rapidly. Some of the jackalopes would be going out later to sing near cowboy campfires under the stars. But now was a time for early rest and relaxation.

As the others were leaving the prairie, Molly decided to visit her friend the Ginkgo tree. She regretted she had not taken time to say hello that morning. As she approached, Molly listened to a pair of hoot owls calling back and forth among the trees up on the hill. It was mealtime for them, too. The shape of the Ginkgo tree loomed before her in the dusk.

Suddenly, what had appeared to be one form, divided into two, and she realized that someone else was there.

"Well, I swear by Guinevere's ghost, if it isn't Molly!" Old Grandal hopped out from under the branches of the tree and chuckled, "Actually, I was waiting for you."

"How. . . ," Molly stopped before completing the question. With Grandal, one always could expect the unexpected. So, she said instead, "It's good to see you, Grandal. I've been wondering if you have been back over to Thunder Mountain since our trip that time."

"Oh, yes, several times. I try to include that in my rounds occasionally."

Molly thought she detected a faint smile on Grandal's face, but it was difficult to tell in the gloomy darkness. Also, he was wriggling his nose, and even put his paw up to rub it as though it itched.

"Well, did you see that coyote we helped get out of the trap? I think you were going to call him Traynor."

"Yes, Molly, I have seen Traynor three times. His leg healed, but he will always have a limp. It doesn't keep him from running, but just not as fast as he did before." Grandal looked appraisingly at the jackalope.

"That should be good for creatures like us, Grandal. Do you think he remembers you and me?"

"I don't have any doubt about it. Some of his kind apparently have long memories. . . aye, and the cunning of Merlin." The last, Grandal spoke as an aside to himself.

Molly wasn't sure just how to take Grandal's words sometimes. It was a bit mystifying. But apparently Grandal was satisfied that the crippled coyote over at Thunder Mountain was not one they should worry about. But the others, that was a different story. She told him about the experience in the box canyon and about seeing a coyote on the hillside. When she had finished, the old jack rabbit didn't reply for a minute. He tipped his notched ear forward and straightened it again. He rubbed his nose on the trunk of the tree. He made a little sound in his throat like coughing, or chuckling. She couldn't tell which. Finally, Grandal seemed to regain his voice.

"It's good to be careful and on the alert, Molly. Life is not always an easy path for us creatures in this country. I know we have enemies, but I think you are learning also. . . that things are not always what they seem!" With these words, Grandal tipped his ear again at her, hopped over the top of the rock pile under the tree and seemed to evaporate in the growing dusk. Strain her eyes as she must, Molly could not see his form or any sign of movement among the jumble of rocks, bushes and shadows beyond. "Well, just like that again! He didn't even wait for a good-bye." She had almost forgotten that the Ginkgo tree was there to hear her, and was surprised when it spoke.

"Grandal is like that, Molly. We have to get used to it."

"Gosh, you are right here! I'm sorry I didn't take time to talk with you when I came by today." Molly moved over a little farther from the rock pile because one of the rat snakes had just come back from hunting and wanted to go into its hole.

"It's okay I guess you had a good reason to be in such a hurry." The tree's whispering voice could barely be heard above the breeze that came and rustled among its leaves, some of which had already changed color and fallen to the ground. Molly used her teeth to pick up a twig with leaves that had fallen and transferred it to her two paws. Sitting back on her haunches, she began to talk.

"I was pretty frightened. Well, you heard me telling Grandal about the coyote I saw."

"Yes, I heard it. Being a tree, I don't have to worry about coyotes, but I can sympathize with you."

Molly put her nose down and sniffed the leaves on the twig. They were almost dry, and tickled her nose. "It is very hard for me to understand that old jack rabbit sometimes. I couldn't tell if he really believed me or not. It almost seemed like he wanted to laugh at me."

The Ginkgo tree seemed to sigh (or was it just a creaking from the wind?). "Grandal has his secrets. I'm sure I don't understand them either. I don't even know how old he is."

"I've wondered about that, too," Molly replied. "It seems he knows about things from long, long ago. He would have to be very old."

"Well, he looked old the first time I ever saw him," the tree confided. "I was just a small sapling then. That was many summers back." The two were quiet for a moment, and Molly reflected on the many unusual experiences she remembered having with Grandal. She had to admit to herself that the outcomes had usually been good. But it was frustrating not to understand why certain things were happening until after they happened.

This business about "things not always being what they seemed," for example. It was certainly a strange thing for Grandal to say. She knew very well what she had heard while she was in the little box canyon and what she had seen on the way home. Indeed, that was not an imaginary coyote! Molly was so absorbed in her thoughts that she forgot that the Ginkgo sprig was still between her paws.

"I'm glad that you like my leaves." The tree's whisper was almost a chuckle. "The rest will be falling soon, and you can have those too if you want them."

"Oh, no! There is really nothing I can do with them." Molly put the sprig down with some embarrassment. "But they are quite beautiful in the daylight with their fall colors."

"Thank you," murmured the tree. "I wish I could keep them on during the cold winter for a little cover, but that's not the way it is."

"I wish you could keep them, too. . . at least until spring. But then you would have to drop them to make room for new ones."

The jackalope stayed with her friend for a few more minutes. Then, she said, "good night," and retired to the family burrow where the others were already asleep. But slumber didn't come easily as Molly recalled the strangeness of the coyote howls that morning while she was singing in the little canyon. She still had an eerie feeling thinking about it. But finally a fitful sleep did come, and Molly dreamed that she was at a place near the evil oasis, Matamor. *Coming off the slope into the plain, she seemed to cross an invisible line, and*

Matamor's magnetic power gripped her like a giant hand. She had no strength to resist. As she was being drawn closer and closer to the deadly paradise, a monstrous beast appeared and stood at the edge of the woods waiting for her with red glaring eyes and gaping jaws. She awoke in terror to find herself safe and sound there in the dark coziness of the burrow.

"This will not do," she whispered to herself. *"It's silly of me to let myself be so disturbed like this."* So, with a valiant effort, Molly finally turned her thoughts to more pleasant things. She snuggled closer to the slumbering members of her family and shortly was fast asleep.

The next morning, Molly was late coming out of the burrow. Nearby, several of her family and neighbors were talking about a new cattle herd and cowboy camp that had recently located to the north . This meant new ears to hear some of the jackalope songs. For several pranksters in the group, it meant opportunities for tricks that could be played on new, unsuspecting cowboys. For some of those, a jackalope's voice might still be novel. Old Uncle Eps, a veteran of many a campfire escapade in his youth, was nearby regaling some eager listeners with one of his tales.

"Yep, there I wuz in the bushes with my friends, a singing to them folks by the fire. One of the cowpokes wuz kinda short and had a limp. I believe the others called him 'Stumpy.' Well, Stumpy liked my singing so much that he got out his harmonica and wuz playing right along."

At this point, Uncle Eps stopped to shake his grizzled, gray head at a clownish young jackalope that had sat up on his haunches. With his paws, the imp was imitating the playing of a harmonica.

"Just you wait, Jasper! One of these nights you're gonna be into that deviltry, and a big owl'll swoop down with his talons and carry you right off! Them antlers'll just give him somepin' to hold on to."

The old jackalope wasn't about to be deterred from his storytelling, however. Since he couldn't go on the evening expeditions any longer, his greatest pleasure came from telling stories from the past.

"Well, I decided to find out what would happen if I stopped a singing. So, I did that, an' that Stumpy , he kep' on a playin'. Right good harmonica music, it was, too. But I wuz gonna have me a little fun, so I started imitating his music a little, and then right in the middle of his tunes, I'd let out a loud giggle. That went on for a little while, and I could see that Stumpy wuz a getting madder an' madder. The other cowboys wuz a shuffling around and laughing at ol' Stumpy whiles he wuz still a tryin' to play. Finally, I snuk up as close to the campfire as I could without them seeing me and let out an extra loud giggle."

"What happened then, Uncle Eps?" Even Jasper's attention was now riveted to the story.

"You know, that Stumpy wuz so mad, he stood up and flung that harmonica right out toward where I wuz. When it hit the bush in front of me, dogged if it didn't get hung up in the branches. When I saw where it wuz, I reached in there with my teeth, sorta fast-like, grabbed that harmonica and skedaddled outa there."

"Golly! The cowboys didn't even see you?"

"Nope." Uncle Eps gave a raspy chuckle. "Well, I held on to that thing and carried it back home with me. Stumpy probably wuz out a lookin' for it the next day. . . musta decided it got carried off by a pack rat."

His audience roared with laughter, and Jasper even did a couple of somersaults in his glee.

"That's not the end of it." Uncle Eps' old eyes glowed with the memory. "The next day, I messed around with that harmonica, holding it with my paws and trying to blow on it. Finally, I could get a couple of notes out. So that night, we went back to the campfire. While the others wuz a singing, I started playing on the harmonica. You should have seen them

cowpokes when they heard that. Stumpy musta known that wuz his harmonica, 'cause in a minute he had his pistol out and wuz a shootin' off into the dark where we wuz and yelling about 'getting that dadburned varmint.' We didn't waste no time in getting out of there!"

It seemed no one else could top Uncle Eps' story. The young bucks were now pumped up with enthusiasm and could hardly wait until nightfall to visit the new cowboys' campfire. For the rest of the morning, the pranksters in the group plotted and sniggered over the tricks they hoped to play. Meanwhile, some of the older jackalopes could only shake their heads and comment sadly on the downfall of the new generation.

"I don't know what the world's coming to. All these young ones want to do is play games and tricks. It's not like it was when we were their age." Old Jenny Jackalope was talking to her neighbor, Matilda.

"That's the truth, Jenny. Why, I remember when singing for the cowboys was a serious thing. It is a responsibility that all jackalopes have in life. If we played around like these young ones do now, our elders would give us a good thumping."

"I know it, Matilda. That rascal, Eps! He never was up to much good when he was younger. Now, he's just putting foolishness into the heads of those scamps out there!"

Jenny looked around carefully to see if other ears were listening, then spoke confidentially in a lower tone. "I can tell you this about Eps. . . and a couple of the others, too. When they were young, I remember they used to sneak off and nibble on loco weed. They didn't think anybody ever knew it, but I saw them doing it."

"You don't mean that, Jenny! That would have made a great scandal if it had gotten out. . . almost as bad as the time when Priscilla's grandmother fell into a gopher hole after drinking too much cactus juice!" And so it went. The young ones cavorted and plotted, while the older ones talked about the times long before when things were much better.

For a while, Molly observed the little groups clustering here and there in their play and their conversations. Finding a certain boredom with it all, she finally hopped a little way out onto the prairie and found her friend, Fraida, picking some seeds from the cone of a scrub pine.

"*Ha, ha*, good to see you, Mollylope! *Chiga, chiga*, nice day, *chiga, chiga*." The magpie was in good spirits evidently.

"I'm happy to see you, Fraida. It sounds like you are feeling good about something." Molly knew her friend pretty well.

"Ya can say that again, *chiga, chiga*. Found me a place, *chiga, chiga*, over at that new cowboys' camp. Plenty of cows there, got lotsa bugs and ticks, *chiga, chiga*." The black-and-white bird spied a small beetle on the tree trunk and darted after it. "Gotcha! Now, what was I a saying, Mollylope? *Chiga, chiga*. Oh, yes, the cowboys' camp. Great place, *chiga, chiga*."

"That's good news, and I'm glad you found that place, Fraida." Molly watched the bird's beak as it dug again between the opening petals of the cone. "I wanted to ask you, have you seen that coyote again, the one you told me about the other day?"

"Seen one or two, *chiga, chiga*. Not sure about the same one. What's the difference? *Chiga, chiga*, they're all coyotes. Mangy creatures, too, *chiga, chiga*."

"Well, I was just wondering." Molly decided to change the subject. "Some of the other jackalopes are going over to that new camp tonight. They're planning to have a lot of fun and stay most of the night. What is it like over there?"

"Good place, Mollylope, *chiga, chiga*. Got some trees and grass around. . ." The magpie suddenly stopped and eyed her friend. "Don't know about you jackalopes, *chiga, chiga*. There's something I better tell you, *chiga, chiga*."

Molly said nothing and stared at Fraida.

"That camp, it's close to Matamor. Just over the ridge, in the next valley, *chiga, chiga*. Just thought you better know, *chiga, chiga*." *"Matamor!"* A sudden chill visited the jackalope. The others apparently didn't realize the two places were that close. She addressed the magpie in a loud voice, "Fraida, are you sure about this? Did you feel anything unusual when you were there at the camp?"

"Nope, not a thing, *chiga, chiga*. Of course, I'm a bird, and Matamor doesn't call me like it does you little animals, *chiga, chiga*. I know it was Matamor, *chiga, chiga*. Saw it myself."

Nodding, Molly decided to leave the magpie with her seed hunting and started back to find some of the other jackalopes. Hurrying along, and preoccupied with her thoughts, Molly almost bumped into Priscilla who was eyeing some green leaves just out of her reach on a large shrub.

"Oh, hi, Molly." Her cousin gave her a casual glance. "I saw you out there talking to that crow. Why do you waste your time with a silly bird such as her?"

"Fraida's not a crow. She is a magpie, and sometimes she makes a lot of sense," Molly replied.

"Well, to me, she's a low kind of creature, always chitter-chattering. Why don't you just tell her to leave and go sit on a cow's rump and eat bugs?"

"She's my friend, Priscilla."

Priscilla gave a disdainful toss of her head. "Some friend! But I guess none of us should be surprised. You have some strange habits, Molly, like talking to trees and going off by yourself. Why don't you act normal and do the things the other jackalopes do?"

"Well, I guess each of us does the things she thinks are important. And for me, those are different than the things you think about." Molly wanted to say more, but decided to hold her tongue.

"I think it's important to try to be somebody, Molly. Have some pride in yourself. Here you are, practically grown, and you don't seem to care at all about how you look, or what the others say about you."

Molly was slow with her answer. "No. . . I guess I don't think much about that anymore. It just seems. . . ." Then she decided to change the subject and ask a question. "Priscilla, have you ever heard of an old jack rabbit named Grandal?"

"No" was the prompt reply. "I've never heard the name around here." Then she added sarcastically, "I guess that is another of your peculiar friends."

"He is that, most definitely! Well, good-bye, Priscilla." Molly hopped away, leaving her stylish cousin staring at her a bit perplexed.

During the rest of the day, Molly talked with several of the jackalopes who were planning to go on the excursion that night. She told them what the magpie had said about Matamor being just over a ridge from the cowboys' new camp. A few of them listened to her seriously and said they were glad to know it and would be careful. The others laughed and said that with a ridge in between, they would be safe enough. She was told not to be a worrywart. One of the jackalopes she told was Jumbo who had decided he wanted to make the trip. His only response was, "Matamor, *huh*? I've heard it has some delicious plants. But I guess the old folks say we shouldn't go there." He wandered away to eat at another clump of grass.

When the moon rose that night, a large group of jackalopes left the village and headed out on their big adventure. It was

a clear night, and everybody's spirits were high. Some were already humming little medleys of song as they hopped away. Young Jasper could hardly contain his excitement over a superb trick that he and his friends had thought up. He jumped and cavorted about. There were catcalls, laughter and a general chorus of voices as the happy animals scurried up the slope. Molly could hear the sounds long after the last forms were visible in the moonlight, merging into the brush and shadows above the village.

For the jackalopes that remained in the village, the night was uneventful. They all retired fairly early to their burrows and enjoyed an uninterrupted sleep. Rays from a rising sun were just beginning to peek through the rocks, cactus and shrubby plants when the first of the excursion party returned.

"The others are right behind us," one called, "but two are missing!" As more from the party streamed in, everybody seemed to talk at once. Molly stood out on the edge of the group listening intently to the jangle of voices.

"It was Jumbo and that Abigail that follows him around."

"We didn't miss 'em at first. I thought they were back behind me somewhere."

"Well, last time I saw them was right after we left the cowboys' camp."

"Oh, they probably stopped off to eat. You know Jumbo."

"You're right. They'll be along in a little bit."

As the talk went on, Molly felt a growing sense of alarm. She approached one of the returnees and asked him, "While you were at the cowboys' camp, could you feel anything from Matamor, being that close to it?"

"Well, I felt a bit of a pull," the other answered, "but it wasn't strong, and I knew where it was coming from. Besides, we were all having a wonderful time." He looked at Molly with his eyes dancing. "You should have been there! Jasper's trick had those cowboys chasing out into the dark in all directions."

"I'm sorry to have missed it," Molly replied. But as the group was breaking up, she couldn't escape a nagging feeling of uneasiness. About five minutes later, she caught sight of a bird swooping in from the same direction of the returned excursion party. A sun's ray flashed on its black and white feathers, and Molly recognized Fraida. The magpie alighted on the top of a nearby shrub.

"Bad news, Mollylope, *chiga, chiga*. That Jumbo and silly Abigail are headed toward Matamor! *Chiga, chiga*, I saw 'em going up the ridge in that direction."

"So that's it!" Molly exclaimed. "I was afraid of something like that. When did you see them?"

"Just a little bit after the others left, *chiga chiga*. What's to do about it? I knew I couldn't stop 'em, *chiga, chiga*. Jumbo won't listen to me." Fraida shifted her balance on the perch.

"I don't know what to do. . . let me think a minute." Molly realized that it might be too late for any of the other jackalopes to try and save the errant two. Could she even persuade anyone to make the attempt? Everyone had been told the dangers of getting too close to Matamor. In her perplexity, Molly wandered away and left her friend searching for insects among the shrubs. Standing near a rock and gazing absently at the horizon, she searched inward for an answer. "*What to do, what to do? If only Grandal could be here to advise me.*" But no sooner was the thought fully formed, than a voice spoke nearby.

"You must go, Molly. Take some others with you."

It was Grandal's voice. Molly looked around. No one was there, just the same brown soil, rocks, shrubs and the blue sky above. Then the voice continued, "That is the right thing to do. But again I must tell you, there will be real danger. Always use your head and your courage." Again, there was a pause, then, "Remember the last thing I said to you over at the Ginkgo tree!" There was silence.

"I don't know how he did that. But I'm sure it was Grandal." She spoke aloud to herself. "Well, there's no choice now. Some of us have to go." Molly hopped back quickly to the magpie.

"Fraida, I am going to try to get some others to go with me. Maybe, we can get over there in time to talk to Jumbo before they get too close to Matamor. Will you go with us to act as a scout?"

"No problem, Mollylope, *chiga, chiga*. But we'd better hurry, *chiga, chiga*."

"I know." As she rushed off to tell the others, it was with the thought that Jumbo, after the night's festivities, would probably be quite hungry. Hopefully, he and Abigail would be stopping often to eat. If so, there just might be enough time to reach them.

A short time later, Molly found herself struggling to keep up with four of the bravest and strongest jackalopes from the village. There was no need for a larger group. At times, she found herself falling behind, but always in close attendance by the faithful magpie who kept up a steady stream of comment and encouragement.

"On up this way, Mollylope, *chiga, chiga*. I can see the others. They just went past those two juniper trees up there, *chiga, chiga*."

Molly saved her breath for the effort she was making.

"*Chiga, chiga*, not far to the cowboys' camp now, *chiga, chiga*. That greedy Jumbo! Thinking about food alla' time. Matamor's gonna teach 'em! *Chiga, chiga*."

They finally passed the cowboys' camp and their cattle herd. The magpie settled for a moment on a rock and looked longingly at the grazing cows in the distance. Then she flew up past the group of jackalopes to the top of the ridge. Shortly, she returned. "Nope, didn't see 'em on this side or on the top, *chiga, chiga*. Musta crossed over. Hurry, hurry! *Chiga, chiga*."

The four in the front had halted briefly to allow Molly to catch up and to hear Fraida's report. "Well, we've gotta keep moving. When we get to the top, we should be able to see Matamor. How're you coming, Molly?"

Molly answered the speaker in a rasping voice while panting to catch her breath, "Okay. . . I guess. It's alright if you go on ahead. I'll get there. . . somehow."

So the would-be rescuers resumed their march and moved up the slope as rapidly as each could travel among the rocks, cactus and stubby trees. At the top, Molly found the other four waiting for her and gazing into the valley below. She, too, found herself staring, almost mesmerized by the sight. A small plain lay between the bottom of the slope below them and the most beautiful oasis any of them could ever imagine. The tops of stately palm trees stood majestically above verdant gardens and groves of green. The sunlight shimmered on a small lake near the center, and a vision of its cool and inviting waters appealed mightily to the thirsty travelers. They could almost taste the sweetness of the luxuriant plants visible there under the palms. Here on the crest of the ridge, the pull was very strong. But still, each of the jackalopes in the party knew the danger, and their wills were strong enough to withstand the pull. Jumbo and Abigail were not in sight.

"Probably, it's too late," one of the front four said, "they may already be inside the oasis." However, just as he spoke,

the figures of Jumbo and Abigail emerged from some trees just down below them, and started to move out onto the plain.

"It's them! Quick! Maybe we can get down there soon enough to call them back." As the party started to descend the slope, they could also see a gray form leave some brush near the edge of the oasis and slink into the green foliage. "*Ha*," said Molly bitterly to herself, "Another coyote or wolf heading in for the kill."

The rescuers hastened down the ridge. At the bottom, they peered out from among the rocks and shrubs onto the little, open plain. There were Jumbo and Abigail in full view over near the edge of the oasis.

"A little closer, and we'll call to them." Five courageous jackalopes stepped out onto the plain, accompanied by the watchful magpie.

Jumbo and Abigail entered through the green curtain of the oasis together, almost at a run. "*Ah!*" Jumbo breathed audibly. "This is wonderful. What did I tell you! Everything looks so good that I don't know where to start first." He snatched a huge mouthful from the first clump of luscious green grass he saw. Behind him, Abigail wasted no time in attacking the tender leaves of a large, dense shrub. For a moment, the two feasted in complete bliss. Even their smallest fears were forgotten. Around them were the sounds of songbirds and the aromas of even sweeter plants yet. It was truly paradise on earth!

Jumbo reached for another bite—and heard a bloodcurdling scream behind him! Whirling around, he saw Abigail recoiling backward from the awful sight of a large, savage, beastly head thrusting through the branches of the shrub, its baleful eyes gleaming and jaws open wide to reveal deadly, pointed teeth. There was a terrible growl followed by a squeal

from Jumbo. After that, terror paralyzed their vocal chords, and they fled desperately.

As Molly followed the others out beyond the rocks and scrub and onto the plain, she felt a sudden change. Some new force was taking control of her body and impelling her toward the oasis. She realized with an inward shock that this was the same feeling she had during the nightmare, only now it was no dream. This was reality, a deadly reality that now had her and her companions in its grip. As they were pulled forward, the figures of Jumbo and Abigail far ahead of them were disappearing into the foliage of the oasis. But to Molly, it no longer seemed to matter. The appeal of the oasis itself was quickly overwhelming her reasoning ability. Its voice was speaking to her, soothing and promising. Soon she would have no desire to resist. Overhead, Fraida flew in frantic circles, calling on them to stop, but her warning went unheeded. Steadily, they moved forward toward Matamor like mindless robots.

Then came a sudden disturbance at the edge of the oasis. Jumbo and Abigail half tumbled in their haste to get out of the shrubbery with a large, vicious coyote at their heels. The three seemed embroiled in the same cloud of dust. The shock of what was happening awakened Molly and her companions, and they stopped, frozen in their tracks. In horror, she could see the coyote gaining on the lumbering and struggling Jumbo while Abigail surged ahead. Then, Jumbo stumbled and fell. Molly closed her eyes and whispered, "*He's a goner now!*" But when she reopened her eyes, the pudgy jackalope had miraculously regained his footing, and the

coyote was again running behind him. They could hear the snarls and snapping of its teeth.

"Run! There's nothing we can do. Run!" someone shouted. The five would-be rescuers turned and fled for the slope. Each was on his or her own. Molly was quickly outdistanced by the four. In seconds, Abigail swept by, her mouth open and eyes filled with terror. "*Why did I ever get myself into this,*" Molly thought to herself as she ran. "*It may be the end! If he doesn't get Jumbo, he'll probably get me.*" She frantically tried to get to the hillside. Perhaps, up among the rocks and trees, she would have a chance to hide somewhere.

As Molly stumbled in among the first scrubby bushes at the bottom of the slope, she became aware of a sound. Slowing her pace to listen, she realized that the coyote was howling—some distance behind her. As soon as she could find the cover of a bush and look back, Jumbo came staggering past, wheezing and gasping as he continued desperately upward. But just below, about twenty yards out on the plain, the coyote was sitting down and looking up in her direction. Again, it tilted its head back and howled, a lonesome, melancholy sound. Molly's breath caught in her throat. It was the same sound she had heard in the canyon that day when she became so frightened. There was something very strange happening here. Why hadn't this coyote followed her and Jumbo up the slope? He certainly could have caught Jumbo, who couldn't have run much farther. And while she was looking around and thinking, the coyote stood up and trotted off a few steps and stopped. It was then that she realized, for the first time, that its right, front leg was crippled! Molly sat in a state of shock, as as a wave of revelation surged through her mind. Grandal had said, "Things are not always what they seem." Finally, she understood what he had meant. The coyote she was now seeing was Traynor, the one she had helped save from the trap! Traynor, the crippled coyote! It was him that had been standing on the hill watching the jackalope village. It was him that accompanied her singing when she was in the canyon. Today, in the only way he knew how, Traynor had managed to save her whole party from a terrible fate in the depths of Matamor. All this time, she had been so distrusting and frightened! Now, as the fear left her, it was like she was emerging free from a suffocating blanket. Molly left the bush and hopped out into the open so the coyote could see her.

When he saw the jackalope with one antler move into the open area, Traynor gave a little prancing step in recognition.

Molly, hardly realizing she was doing it, gave a curious little hop in return. Then the crippled coyote seemed to nod to her and trotted off in the direction of Thunder Mountain. Molly watched him for a long time. As she finally turned to resume her trek up the slope, Fraida flew over from the top of a small oak tree.

"*Chiga, chiga*, mighty happy you're okay, Mollylope! *Chiga chiga*, that was a strange coyote. . . yes, strange indeed. Kinda acted like he knew you."

"You're right, Fraida. He did know me. . . all the time he was there." The two friends continued their journey homeward. At the top of the slope, they again found the others waiting for them.

As the weeks went by, Molly found herself occasionally going far out into the hills and the prairie at night and singing under the open sky. Traynor often came to a nearby spot when she was there. She would hear his howl reaching upward toward the glittering stars and the friendly moon in concert with her voice. Then she would again feel a sense of magic as she did that night with the sheepherder and his flute. It seemed that in those moments, her spirit and Traynor's spirit were truly joined. She was never afraid again.

Many Years Later

As the years passed, the western part of the country underwent dramatic changes. With the coming of the automobile, paved roads soon followed the railroads that had arrived earlier. Towns and cities grew as more people moved to the west to live. The days of the great cattle herds on the open plains, cowboys on horseback, frontier mining towns, and gunfights all became a part of the past. Memories of those times are rich and colorful. The vast western plains, deserts, canyons, rugged mountains, and wildlife were unlike any others in the country. People began coming by train, bus and automobile from the eastern cities and other parts of the country to visit the west and enjoy its splendor. Dude ranches became popular. Guided tours were a frequent way for visitors to see some of the more remote areas.

It was just such a group that made its way one afternoon on horseback to a campsite at the foot of Thunder Mountain. There were two married couples in their thirties, along with a single man who was a senior business partner with the other men. Their guide was much older, perhaps in his early seventies, with a kind of toughness about him that spoke of many years spent out of doors. Despite his age, he had been highly recommended. No other guide, it was said, knew this part of the region as well.

Their camp was soon set-up next to a small creek. By nightfall, the group had finished their meal and was lounging around the glowing coals of the cooking fire, enjoying mugs of hot coffee. It was a beautiful desert night, although small gusts of wind occasionally rustled the needles and leaves of the pine and oak trees nearby. The old guide brought several more sticks of deadwood to the fire and busied himself with building it into a comforting glow.

"That old gold mine over on the other side of the mountain. You said its been abandoned for a long time?" The business partner's question was really intended as a way of getting the old man to talk again. Since arriving at the campsite, the guide had said little, answering most previous questions in monosyllables.

"Yep, its been a long time." The old man stood up from tending the fire and rubbed the back of his neck.

"I wonder who first discovered that mine." The partner continued to pursue the subject.

"Well, can't rightly say fer shore, but I heard a couple of men from Arkansas wuz prospectin' thet side of the mountain back in the seventies. If it wuz them, they didn't git much gold."

"Why was that?" one of the other men asked.

"Thar used to be a tale about the Spanish comin' from Mexico an' mining gold in these parts." The guide was now warming to the subject. "They mighta done thet because I heard the mine wuz already thar when the Arkansas men came. It wuz 'bout wore out."

"I think it is sad." The smaller of the women glanced at her husband as she spoke. "Most of the gold mines are gone, or at least nobody is working them now. The buffalo and the wolves are just about extinct. We haven't seen any cowboys on this trip. Pretty soon, all that will be left, will just be the stories."

"Well, ma'am, I kinda feel thet way myself at times. I kin remember when thar wuz sheepherders along with the cattle an' more wild critters. Thar wuzn't scarcely a night when yuh couldn't hear them coyotes a howling." The old guide's tone was wistful.

"Coyotes!" the woman's husband joined in. "We haven't heard a single one so far."

"Thar's a few left, but a lot of 'em been killed out," the guide replied. "I remember we use'ta trap 'em when I wuz young. One of 'em got away one time. . . kinda strange, too. . . ," and his voice trailed off, then returned. "People used to say this here mountain wuz haunted by a coyote ghost. They'd see 'im or hear 'im up thar. It wuz a crippled coyote, they said."

"A coyote ghost!" The two women spoke almost at the same time, and the small one continued, "Tell us more about that."

"Ain't too much to tell, ma'am. Folks thet saw it said it would jest appear sometimes, runnin' along with it's crippled leg, or maybe jest a standin' out on a rock. It looked all misty like, then it would disappear—jest like thet!"

"Did you ever see it?"

"No, ma'am, can't say thet I ever did fer shore. I thought maybe, one time. But, I use ta hear it a howlin' sometimes—it sounded all mournful. An' some folks thet heard it claimed thet they could hear somebody a singing off out in tha prairie. . . at night."

One of the men looked skeptical. "I thought the prairie looked pretty open this afternoon. Are there any people living out there?"

"Nope, not fer miles. But a few folks thought it must hev been a jackalope."

"This is getting rich!" exclaimed the small woman. "A jackalope! Are you talking about that mythical creature? Wasn't it supposed to resemble a jack rabbit and have horns like an antelope?" She leaned over to her husband and whispered, "Honey, I love these old tales and superstitions. We just have to come back out here next year!"

"Well, ma'am, thet's what they say it looks like. But I ain't never seen one myself." The old man lapsed into silence, his reservoir of speech seemingly exhausted. He bent back down to the fire, poked it briefly with a stick and sat staring into the flames. At times, the others thought they heard him mutter something to himself.

The tourists continued talking. They had three more days before their trip would be over, and they would have to head back east. Perhaps next year, they could come back to this same area. There were so many places they had not seen, and so many old legends to uncover. There was something in the atmosphere out here that was exhilarating. It aroused one's yearning to explore, to keep riding from one ridge to the next, and to drink in all of the beautiful scenery and wonderful stories. It was a pity time was so short.

The old man was sitting by the fire watching the flames as they became lower and lower until most of the light came only from the glow of red coals. He seemed bemused and detached from the condition of the fire itself and from the conversation around him. Then suddenly, something startled him, and he jumped to his feet, cupping one hand to his ear. From the direction of the prairie, he heard the unmistakable voice of a woman singing, pure and clear. The voice had a frequent lilt to it like the sound of a flute that added to its beauty and charm. A look of amazement and disbelief came over his face.

"It's thet woman agin! Ya'll listen! But. . . can't hardly believe. . . it's been nigh forty-five years now!"

The others stared at their old guide as he then swung his head around toward the mountain.

"An' tha' crippled coyote! He's up thar now. I kin hear him real good." He turned toward his listeners.

"Doncha hear that? He's howling all lonesome and strange like." His attention then returned to the voices that were coming from the mountain and the prairie. The visitors watched the old man, standing by a dying campfire while the wind gently stirred the pines and chased a wisp of a cloud across the face of the moon.

"I guess what he hears is the wind up there in the trees," whispered one of the men; and, the others nodded. Then the partner spoke, and his voice was a little louder.

"Old Jake has been living by himself alone in these hills for too long. I think we need to get ourselves a new guide next year."

". . . Heard melodies are sweet, but those unheard
Are sweeter; therefore, ye soft pipes, play on;
Not to the sensual ear, but, more endeared,
Pipe to the spirit ditties of no tone. . . ."

—*From* Ode On a Grecian Urn
by John Keats